'Are you as[k] *mistress?'* D[esirée cried]
out.

A decidedly sensuous smile curved Sebastian's lips. 'Would that be so terrible? I would never hurt you, sweetness. Indeed, I would be exceedingly gentle and give you all that a woman could ask for.'

His hand moved gently through the water towards her and Desirée gasped as the tips of his fingers brushed lightly across her breast. 'You forget yourself, sir!' she cried, thrusting his hand away. 'And not only in your conduct! How dare you speak to me in such an inappropriate manner?'

'Why? Do you truly find the idea of being my mistress so *very* objectionable?'

A young woman disappears.
A husband is suspected of murder.
Stirring times for all the neighbourhood in

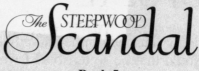
The STEEPWOOD
Scandal

Book 5

When the debauched Marquis of Sywell won Steepwood Abbey years ago at cards, it led to the death of the then Earl of Yardley. Now he's caused scandal again by marrying a girl out of his class—and young enough to be his granddaughter! After being married only a short time, the Marchioness has disappeared, leaving no trace of her whereabouts. There is every expectation that yet more scandals will emerge, though no one yet knows just how shocking they will be.

The four villages surrounding the Steepwood Abbey estate are in turmoil, not only with the dire goings-on at the Abbey, but also with their own affairs. Each story in **The Steepwood Scandal** follows the mystery behind the disappearance of the young woman, and the individual romances of lovers connected in some way with the intrigue.

Regency Drama
intrigue, mischief...and marriage

A MOST IMPROPER PROPOSAL

Gail Whitiker

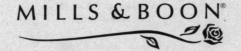

MILLS & BOON®

First published in Great Britain 2001
Harlequin Mills & Boon Limited,
Eton House, 18-24 Paradise Road, Richmond, Surrey TW9 1SR

© Harlequin Books S.A. 2001

Special thanks and acknowledgement are given to Gail Whitiker for her contribution to The Steepwood Scandal series.

ISBN 0 263 82846 8

Set in Times Roman 10½ on 12½ pt.
119-0901-61155

Printed and bound in Spain
by Litografia Rosés S.A., Barcelona

Originally hailing from Pembrokeshire, **Gail Whitiker** now lives on beautiful Vancouver Island on the west coast of Canada. When she isn't indulging her love of writing, you'll find her enjoying brisk walks along the Island's many fine beaches, or trying to catch up on her second love, reading. She wrote her first novel when she was in her teens, and still blesses her English teacher for not telling her how bad it really was.

Look out for
THE GUARDIAN'S DILEMMA
by Gail Whitiker

in **The Steepwood Scandal**
Coming Soon

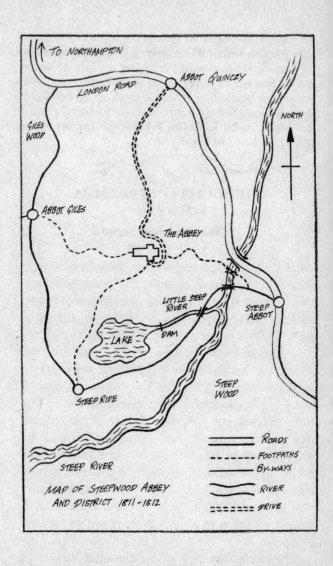

TO NORTHAMPTON

ABBOT QUINCEY

LONDON ROAD

GILES WOOD

NORTH

ABBOT GILES

THE ABBEY

LITTLE STEEP RIVER

STEEP ABBOT

LAKE

DAM

STEEP WOOD

STEEP RIDE

STEEP RIVER

ROADS
FOOTPATHS
BY-WAYS
RIVER
DRIVE

MAP OF STEEPWOOD ABBEY
AND DISTRICT 1811-1812

Chapter One

July, 1811

'*Ut sementem feceris, ita metes,*' Miss Desirée Nash recited for the benefit of the twelve young ladies sitting in front of her. 'Or as the saying is more commonly known, as you sow, so shall you reap. Now girls, you will notice that—yes, Miss Melburry?'

'My grandmama used to say that to me all the time, Miss Nash, but she never told me what it meant.'

Desirée smiled at the nine-year-old's confusion. 'It simply means that everyone is responsible for the way their lives turn out, Jane. For example, if you are kind and considerate to the people you meet, it is likely that you will be treated with the same kindness and consideration in return. After all, if a farmer planted only stones in his field, what could he expect to harvest *but* stones? Now, girls, you will notice that in the pronunciation of the word *feceris,* we put the emphasis on—'

'Miss Nash, why must we trouble ourselves to learn

a language that was spoken by fusty old men over a thousand years ago? Surely it cannot be relevant in today's society?'

This question too originated from the back of the room, but unlike Miss Melburry's, Desirée knew that it had not been raised to clarify a point. The Honourable Elizabeth Perry had made no secret of the fact that she disliked the ancient languages and that she resented the time spent in the learning of them. So there was no doubt in Desirée's mind that the question had been asked not just to express the girl's boredom with the subject, but in an attempt to disrupt the class as well.

'Latin, Miss Perry, is at the root of all civilized language,' Desirée began patiently. 'It provides the very foundations upon which English is based. So it only follows that to have a better understanding of Latin is to have a better understanding of the way we speak.'

'And I am sure that is all very well, Miss Nash, but how is that to help us in our search for a *husband*? My father says that all a lady need concern herself with is how to appear charming and attractive to a gentleman. Surely our time would be better spent in those pursuits than in the memorization of words and phrases typically reserved for barristers and the clergy.'

There was a faint titter of amusement from the tall girl seated next to Elizabeth, but Desirée paid it no mind. Isabel Hewton worshipped Elizabeth Perry and had since the first day of class, but she was not in herself a troublemaker. She simply needed someone of a more domineering nature to follow.

No, it was the rest of the girls Desirée was concerned with, and for whatever reason, they seemed unwilling to take up Elizabeth's cry—for which Desirée could only be thankful. She had no wish to antagonize her young charges. Most of their fathers were wealthy and influential men and Mrs Guarding, the founder and headmistress of the Guarding Academy for Girls, was dependent upon their largesse for her living. For that reason alone, it was accepted by all that in difficult situations it was best to avoid confrontation and to move on in as amiable and tactful a manner as possible.

That particular edict did not always sit well with Desirée, however, especially when it came to the likes of Elizabeth Perry. Desirée found it exceedingly difficult to have her authority undermined by a spoiled young woman who would never utter a single word of Latin—or possibly anything else of intelligence—once she passed beyond these walls.

'I would venture to say that you are correct, Miss Perry,' Desirée replied finally. 'In all likelihood, you will not be required to sprinkle your everyday speech with Latin quotes, or to impress your future husband with your knowledge of their meanings and subtleties. However, *because* of the antiquity of the language and the insight it gives us into the nuances of our own, we feel that the inclusion of Latin in the Guarding curriculum is not only necessary, but vital. Therefore, I suggest that if you do not appreciate the opportunity you have been given to learn the language, you might at least have the good manners to remain silent so that the other young ladies can.'

Desirée had not raised her voice. She knew from experience that to lose one's temper was to lose the advantage and that, upon occasion, a well-delivered reprimand could be just as effective as a scold. But when Elizabeth Perry abruptly got to her feet and glared at her, Desirée knew that the outcome had been much the same. Obviously the viscount's daughter was not used to being spoken to in such a manner and certainly not by a person she deemed to be beneath her in every way.

'I shall not stay here and be treated like this,' the young woman cried. 'I shall speak to my father about you this very day, Miss Nash. Just see if I do not!'

With that, she gathered up her things and stormed out of the room.

A shocked silence followed her departure. The eleven remaining girls glanced at each other while Desirée patiently waited for the sound of Miss Perry's footsteps to fade into the distance. When they had, she slowly began to smile.

'The great philosopher Ovid once said, *rident stolidi verba Latina.* Do any of you know what that means?' At the tentative smiles which appeared on the faces of some of the older girls, Desirée nodded. 'Precisely. Only fools laugh at the Latin language. Now, Miss Chisham, perhaps you would be good enough to translate the phrase, patience is a virtue.'

The class soon settled back into its normal routine and the outburst by Miss Perry was forgotten. But Desirée was not so naïve as to believe that she had heard the last of it. She had no doubt that Miss Perry *would* speak to her father about what had happened today. Or that he in turn would speak to Mrs Guarding; a conversation which would result in a meeting between Desirée and the headmistress, at which time she would be gently reminded of the importance of tact and diplomacy when dealing with some of the school's more difficult students. But since Mrs Guarding had also complimented her on her skills as a teacher and upon her unwavering dedication to the Academy, Desirée could not bring herself to feel unduly concerned about it.

It was an acknowledged fact that the Honourable Elizabeth Perry was a thorn in many of the teachers' sides. Ghislaine de Champlain, the French mistress, had encountered the same resistance when it came to the conjugation of verbs. And poor Henriette Mason, who gave instruction in history and geography, had nearly been reduced to tears by the girl's repeated threats to invoke her father's wrath if she was forced to memorize the names of any more than five of the British colonies.

Personally, Desirée wondered why Lord Perry and his wife had enrolled their daughter in the Guarding Academy for Girls in the first place. The school had a well-deserved reputation for academia and its teachers for attempting to break down the intellectual barriers which faced women in society. Its students were encouraged to speak out against the generally accepted norms and to stand up for their rights and freedoms. Indeed, the school's founder and headmistress, Mrs Eleanor Guarding, was an acknowledged emancipationist, as well as being a noted poet and historian.

That was not to say that the social niceties were not also part of the daily curriculum. Miss Jane Emerson guided the young ladies very nicely through the intricacies of the dance, as well as in the proper way to acquit themselves in polite society. And Miss Helen de Coverdale instructed them in watercolours and Italian. But at the Guarding Academy, it was generally accepted that the more important subjects were those which stretched the limits of a young woman's mind; subjects which, hitherto, had been deemed the exclusive domain of men.

At length, the handbell rang in the hall to signal the end of the session.

'Thank you, ladies, that will be all,' Desirée said. 'Tomorrow, we shall begin to study the writings of Euripedes. Perhaps Miss Perry will deign to join us to hear what words of wisdom *that* fusty old man had to share.'

There was a smattering of giggles as the girls filed out and Desirée knew that she had won the day—at least in the eyes of her pupils. And for now, that was all that mattered. The life of a teacher was seldom easy, and she knew there would always be an Elizabeth Perry waiting to make things difficult. But as long as she could instill the required knowledge in the minds of the pupils who truly did wish to learn, Desirée was content. Some might think that a formidable task, but it was not an impossible one. Certainly her mother had managed to imbue her own teachings with insight and humour. And Papa, bless his soul, had been a clergyman of unusual wit and vivacity. He had made the learning of Latin and Greek an adventure rather than the dull, dry undertaking it could have been.

It was because of her parents that Desirée had never found her studies tedious. She had risen to meet the educational challenges they had set forward and had taken great satisfaction in seeing a language come alive. Unlike Lord Perry, they did not adhere to the belief that all a young lady needed to know was the best way to attract a wealthy husband. Before their untimely deaths, they had impressed upon Desirée the value of understanding other cultures and the importance of exploring the philosophies behind them. They had instilled in her an appreciation for the early societies which had formed the models upon which all other civilizations were based, and she had learned to recognize the wisdom of Pythagoras and Euclid.

'Fusty old men indeed,' Desirée muttered as she walked around the room collecting books and papers. Had Elizabeth Perry but troubled herself to find out, she would have been *shocked* at some of the things those fusty old men did.

Of course, there would never be any need for Miss Perry to actually *use* her education, Desirée reflected wryly. Her immediate challenge upon leaving Guarding's would be to find an eligible gentleman and to marry him as quickly as possible. Unlike Desirée, she would never be called upon to make her own way in the world. And while it was true that Desirée might have been more pleasantly situated had she spent time developing the skills which would have allowed her to go to London and find a husband, it was the education her parents had given her which had proved to be her ultimate salvation.

When both of them had succumbed to illness and Desirée had found herself alone in the world at eighteen, it was not the nicety of her manners which had enabled her to apply for a position at the Guarding Academy for Girls, but rather her extensive knowledge of Greek, Latin and philosophy. It was education, not charm, which had spared her the humiliation of having to appeal to her own family for charity when no such offers had been forthcoming.

Even her late grandfather, a man whom Desirée had barely known, but who had had the wherewithal to help her, had refused to reach out his hand. And all because of some silly argument arising from her mother's insistence on falling in love with a penniless clergyman and then on her marrying him against her father's wishes...

'Have I caught you day-dreaming again, Miss Nash?' came a teasing enquiry from the doorway.

Recognizing the voice, Desirée's features relaxed into a smile. Helen de Coverdale was a fairly recent addition to the staff at the Guarding Academy for Girls, but time notwithstanding, she and Desirée had already become good friends. She was six years older than Desirée, and with her soft brown eyes and long dark hair she was one of the loveliest young women Desirée had ever met. Certainly, she was the only teacher at the Guarding Academy who turned heads wherever she went.

And yet, for all that, Desirée had never seen Helen

so much as *glance* at a passing gentleman. Nor did she talk about her past, except to say that she had come from a good home and that she had once been a pupil at the very institution at which she now taught.

But what had caused her to return to the school at the advanced age of thirty, and to apply to Mrs Guarding for a teaching position, was something that Desirée could only wonder at. She turned now and offered her friend an apologetic glance. 'Helen, forgive me, I had no idea you were there. I was, as you say, quite lost in my thoughts.'

'Yes, I noticed as much, but given the way you were beginning to frown, I thought you might have been grateful for the interruption,' Helen said with a smile. 'Have you been having problems with the Honourable Elizabeth again?'

Desirée glanced at her in surprise. 'How did you know?'

'I saw her heading in the direction of Mrs Guarding's study and she had that *look* in her eye. I think you know the one to which I refer.'

Desirée grimaced. 'All too well. I daresay I shall be called to Mrs Guarding's rooms and taken to task once again for the less than diplomatic way I dealt with her reluctance to participate in class today.'

'Let me guess? Was she once again questioning the usefulness of Latin in everyday life?'

'That, and insinuating that the only subjects that *were* worth studying were those which dealt directly with the arts of attracting and securing an eligible *parti.* You can imagine my response.'

'I can indeed.' An attractive dimple appeared at the

corner of Helen's mouth. 'No wonder Miss Perry was looking so put out.'

'Aggravating child,' Desirée muttered. 'I have often wondered *why* Lord and Lady Perry chose to send her here. If all they required of a school was that it teach their daughter how to dance and manage a gentleman's household, they could easily have sent her to any one of a number of exclusive lady's seminaries in London. Goodness knows, they could well have afforded to.'

'Yes, but perhaps they sent her here *because* they did not wish Elizabeth to be so close,' Helen suggested. 'I seem to recall Mrs Guarding saying that there were some problems between Lady Perry and her daughter. Perhaps it was she who suggested Steep Abbot in the first place.'

'I do not find that in the least surprising,' Desirée commented. 'If the Honourable Elizabeth were my daughter, I would have suggested a school in the wilds of Scotland. Still, I suppose it is no concern of mine. And on such a lovely day, I refuse to let thoughts of her weigh me down. I think that I shall go down to the river and amuse myself there for a while.'

At the mention of the river, Helen's eyes widened in dismay. 'Desirée, never say you are going *swimming* again. You know how Mrs Guarding feels about that.'

'Yes, but I have only been down three times this summer, given the dismal weather we've had, and once autumn is upon us, I shall have no inclination to go at all. And on a warm day like this, what could be better than immersing oneself in the cool, clear waters of a secluded woodland pool?'

'Any number of things to my way of thinking,' Helen murmured. 'And you should think better of it too. You know that Elizabeth Perry will take great pleasure in informing Mrs Guarding of your transgressions if she is lucky enough to catch you at them.'

'No one knows that better than I, Helen dear, but you need have no fear that I shall be discovered. Mrs Guarding has given me extra time in exchange for some work I did at the beginning of the week. And since the girls are still in class, I intend to make good use of it. *Sedit qui timuit ne non seccederat.*'

'Which means?'

'He who feared he would not succeed, sat still.'

Helen tilted her head to one side and said in rapid Italian, *Ella che e impigliata deve essere costretta ad soffrire le conseguenze.'*

This time, it was Desirée who smiled. 'And that means?'

'She who is caught must be made to suffer the consequences. Be careful, Desirée. Sometimes, even the most carefully laid plans go awry,' Helen warned softly. 'And when they do, the consequences can come back to haunt us in the most unexpected of ways.'

The River Steep meandered pleasantly through the pastoral countryside south of the small village of Steep Ride before flowing quietly into the densely forested area known as Steep Wood. It changed course once inside the trees, heading north at a point

just past Bredington, the hunting-lodge owned by
Viscount Wyndham, and took another turn before ex-
iting the woods south of the village of Steep Abbot.
There, it formed in its bend a natural pool that measured some sixty feet across and some ten feet deep.

Desirée had stumbled upon the secluded bathing
spot quite by chance when she had been out walking
earlier in the spring. She had taken a different path
into Steep Wood that day and had wandered further
into the forest than she'd intended. But when she had
found the tranquil glade and the shimmering waters
of its pool, she felt as though she had discovered a
pot of gold at the end of the rainbow. She had quickly
glanced around to make sure that she was completely
alone, and then, confident that no one else was likely
to intrude, had stripped down to her shift and dived
in.

Oh, how blissfully cool and refreshing the water
had felt—and how liberating to swim without having
to worry about anyone watching her! It was much
better than going to the seaside, where there were all
manner of people milling about and one had to put
up with those dreadful bathing-boxes for getting in
and out of the water.

Desirée had splashed about and swum for the better
part of thirty minutes.

Unfortunately, Mrs Guarding had been consider-
ably less pleased when Desirée had finally returned
to the school with her hair dripping wet and damp
spots showing through her clothes. She had told
Desirée exactly what she'd thought of her little escapade. And while she had not forbidden Desirée to

swim in the river, she had certainly left her in no doubt as to what would happen the next time she was caught doing so!

Unfortunately, the lure of the forbidden pool continued to beckon, and Desirée did indeed make several more trips to it. But with each visit she grew more circumspect. She only ventured there when she knew she had time enough to get down and back, *and* when she knew the whereabouts of certain students. She also made sure she kept her hair dry and that she brought extra clothing to wear back to school.

Reaching the edge of the pool now, Desirée stood for a moment to enjoy the special feeling of peace and tranquillity that permeated the glade. She could hear the birds singing in the branches overhead, and smell the delicate perfume of wildflowers and grass all around her. It was such a pleasure to escape from the confines of her everyday life. To break free from the confines of a world where there was always someone watching her; waiting to pronounce her guilty for the slightest breach of propriety. And that really was not fair. Whereas men were allowed every freedom imaginable, women were constrained almost from the moment of birth. Even those who endeavoured to enrich their minds by the study of books were labelled bluestockings and looked down upon by their peers.

Still, there was little she could do to change society as a whole, and, unwilling to harbour such dismal thoughts on such a wonderful day, Desirée blithely cast them—and her clothes—aside. Dressed only in her shift, she made her way towards the edge of the pool. She took care not to lose her footing on the slippery grass and slowly made her way in until she stood about waist-deep in the water. Then, putting her arms together, she pushed off with her legs and competently began to swim across the widest part. Her slender arms cut cleanly through the water, her long legs kicking effortlessly behind.

When she reached the far side of the pool, Desirée gracefully turned and started back. Most of the glade was in shadow, but even so, she was not cold. However, when she spotted a sunny patch of grass close to where she had entered the pool, she decided to head that way, knowing it would help to dry her body more quickly.

As soon as her feet touched the bottom, Desirée stood up and slowly began to emerge from the water. Water poured off her body in silver rivulets, her sodden shift clinging to her breasts and hips like a diaphanous veil. The sun felt gloriously warm on her face and the gentle whisper of the breeze against her bare arms and legs was like a soft caress. She closed her eyes and reached her arms up over her head, stretching her fingers to the sun.

'What vision is this?' a deep voice said suddenly. 'A young Aphrodite rising from the waves? For surely, the goddess herself could not have looked more magnificent.'

The teasing yet undeniably masculine voice shattered the peaceful silence of the glade and caused Desirée to utter a sharp gasp. 'Oh!' Dropping her arms protectively over her chest, she anxiously looked around for the source of the voice. 'Where are you, sir? I demand that you show yourself at once!'

The gentleman did—and as soon as he moved, Desirée realised why she had not seen him. He was sitting in the deep grass no more than thirty feet away from her, but he was hidden in the shadows at the base of a huge oak. And it was immediately evident from his appearance that he too had been enjoying the refreshing waters of the pool. His black hair glistened like polished jet against his head, and his wet shirt clung to a chest and shoulders that were altogether too large for her liking.

Thinking only to conceal her nakedness, Desirée quickly stumbled back into the pool. 'You are no gentleman, sir, to sit and watch a lady in such a state of undress!'

'Perhaps not a gentleman, but a man nonetheless. And one not so foolish as to turn away from the sight of a beautiful woman as God intended her to be seen.'

The fact that the man did not even attempt to hide his enjoyment of her scantily clad body brought the blood rushing to Desirée's cheeks. 'Who are you, sir, and what is your business here?'

'The same as yours. The day is fine, the air is warm, and the waters of the river are refreshingly cool. I succumbed to its pleasures the same as you.'

'But…why did you not speak out when first you saw me?'

'I think I must have been asleep,' he admitted sheepishly. 'The first awareness I had of you was when I awoke to the sound of splashing and looked up to see you halfway across the pool. Then I was afraid to speak out lest I startle you and cause you to drown.'

Desirée snorted. 'I am hardly like to drown, sir.'

'How was I to know that?'

'By watching me swim,' she said in a tone that indicated he must either be blind or simple. 'However, that is no longer of import. What is, is that you remove yourself from my glade at once!'

'*Your* glade?' The man chuckled softly. 'Forgive me, Aphrodite, I was not aware that I was trespassing on *private* property.'

'Well, it isn't private…precisely, but I have every right to ask you to leave.'

'Oh? And why would you think so?' he challenged. 'You are obviously enjoying your day, and I am certainly enjoying mine.'

'I *was* enjoying it until you came along to spoil things,' Desirée told him curtly. 'As to why I am asking you to leave, you must realise that, dressed as I am, I cannot get out of the water.'

The man sat forward and locked his arms around his knees. 'Let me be the first to assure you that I have no objection to the manner of your dress, my dear. As for asking me to leave, surely you would not wish me to endanger my safety by pushing me beyond the limits of my endurance?'

Desirée frowned. 'The limits of your endurance have nothing to do with me, sir, and I am hard pressed to understand why you would bring them up. You look fit enough to me. Surely it would be no great effort to rise, turn and walk away.'

'Ah, but unlike you, fair Aphrodite, I did not walk to this tranquil spot. I swam here from Bredington.'

Desirée gasped. 'From *Bredington*?'

'Yes. And once having reached this peaceful glade, I thought to take the opportunity of both enjoying its beauty, and of catching my breath.'

'You *swam* all the way from the lodge?' Desirée repeated in surprise. Mercy, no wonder he was tired. Viscount Wyndham's hunting-box was more than half a mile away and, as fit as this fellow looked, it was a considerable distance for any man to swim. 'I apologise, sir. I can understand your wish to catch your breath before setting off again. However, it does not excuse your conduct in remaining silent. You should have made yourself known to me as soon as you saw me in the water.'

'If it makes me seem any less of a cad, I did think to say something when you began to emerge, but soon after that, I was lost in such wonder that I was robbed of the ability to speak. I could do naught but watch in reverent silence as a lovely water sprite rose from the woodland pool to dry her tender limbs in the golden warmth of the sun.'

Desirée rolled her eyes. 'That, sir, is the most ridiculous thing I have ever heard, and a true gentleman would not have said it.'

'Ah, but I have already told you that I am not a true gentleman, Aphrodite. And I am beginning to think that you are not a true lady either.'

'I *beg* your pardon!'

'No lady of *my* acquaintance would see fit to divest herself of her clothes in a public place and swim in a manner that would make an Amazon proud.'

Desirée blushed hotly. 'I do *not* swim like an Amazon! And this is hardly a public place.'

'But it is not wholly private either. Therefore it is not impossible that someone might have passed by, as you or I have done today.'

'But in all the times I have come here, I have never—'

'Good Lord, do you mean to tell me that you have been here before and that I have missed the pleasure of your loveliness? Dear me, had I but known, I would have left Wyndham to his sport and gone for a swim to see to mine.'

The insinuation that she had suddenly become his 'sport' was the final straw for Desirée. 'I resent you speaking to me in such a manner, sir, and I demand that you leave here at once!'

The man deliberated upon the idea for a moment, but when at length he spoke, his answer was hardly encouraging. 'Well, I suppose I should be heading back. No doubt Wyndham will be wondering where I am. But tell me, fair Aphrodite, how is it that I have not seen you before? Do you live in one of the quaint little villages hereabouts?'

'I do.'

'And have you a handsome husband and several children at home?'

'I am…not married, sir,' Desirée said stiffly, wondering why was she was even bothering to answer his questions.

'Really?' He sat up a little straighter in the grass. 'You live with your family then? A mother and father perhaps.'

She swallowed hard and glanced away. 'No, my parents are…both gone.'

'Are they indeed? Then…what holds you here, sweetness?'

Desirée had not expected the question, nor the sudden softening of his voice. She might even have told him had not the fear of reprisal kept her silent. For in spite of what she accused him of being—or more correctly of *not* being, Desirée had no doubt that the man sitting opposite her *was* a gentleman. His tone of voice and the manner of his speech left her in no doubt as to his position in life. And the fact that he might well have a wife and children, perhaps even a daughter who was, or might some day be, in attendance at the very school at which she taught, made her think twice about revealing her identity.

Unfortunately, by the time she had formed an evasive answer, the gentleman had reached his own. 'So, there is nothing and no one keeping you here. What a shame. To be so young and so lovely and with no one to appreciate it, is a waste indeed.'

'I do not see it as a waste, sir,' Desirée said, lifting her chin in defiance. 'I have no need of a gentleman's appreciation to make my life worthwhile. I am content with it just as it is.'

'But there is so much more than just contentment to be had from life, Aphrodite,' he told her softly. 'So very much more.' Then, with an alacrity that left Desirée gasping, the man stood up—treating her to a brief glimpse of muscular legs clad in buff-coloured breeches—and dived into the water. He disappeared for a few moments, and then surfaced no more than two feet in front of her.

Dear heavens, what a giant of a man he was! The

width of his shoulders was striking from a distance, but up close, Desirée could see just how ruggedly developed his chest and arms were. There was no doubt that, should he wish it, he would have the advantage of her on land *or* in the water.

Desirée gasped and stumbled backwards, struggling to get out of the pool.

'No, wait!' he urged, quickly reaching for her arm.

The hand that closed around her wrist was like iron. 'Let me go, sir!' Desirée cried, trying not to sound as alarmed as she felt.

'If I do, will you stop floundering about like a freshly landed fish and listen to what I have to say?'

The less than flattering description did nothing to lessen the colour in Desirée's cheeks, but it did serve to bring her struggles to a halt. 'I make no promises, sir. How do I know that you do not intend to take advantage of the situation?'

'Because I give you my word as a gentleman that I will not. You have nothing to fear from me, Aphrodite,' the man said softly. 'All I wish from you is a moment's conversation.'

For some reason, Desirée believed him. Though she was woefully inexperienced when it came to men, she did not see the darkness of lust in his eye. But she knew that he was studying her. She saw his eyes drop down below the waterline and knew that she might as well have been wearing nothing at all for what little protection the shift was giving her.

'By God, you're a beauty,' he whispered huskily. 'You have a body that was made to be loved. Come, Aphrodite, let me take you back to London with me.

I shall show you a life unlike any you have ever known. You will have a comfortable house with a maid to attend you and servants to do your bidding. I shall dress you in fine clothes and give you pretty jewels to wear. And all I ask in return is a few hours of sweet pleasure for us both.'

Desirée stared at him, speechless with shock. *Take her back to London with him?* But…surely he was not suggesting…that is, was it possible that he was saying…

'Are you asking me to be…your *mistress*?' she finally gasped out.

A decidedly sensuous smile curved his lips. 'Would that be so terrible? I would never hurt you, sweetness. Indeed, I would be exceedingly gentle and give you all that a woman could ask for.'

His hand moved slowly through the water towards her and Desirée gasped as the tips of his fingers brushed lightly across her breast. 'You forget yourself, sir!' she cried, thrusting his hand away. 'And not only in your conduct! How dare you speak to me in such an inappropriate manner!'

'Why? Do you truly find the idea of being my mistress so *very* objectionable?'

'I do indeed! You are sadly mistaken if you think that the lure of fine clothes and jewels would be enough to tempt me into becoming your courtesan. Did Cleopatra go with Caesar merely because of his wealth? Did Isolde spurn her beloved Tristan for a king's gold?'

The man quirked one dark eyebrow in surprise.

'What's this? My beautiful water sprite possessed of a learned mind as well as an enchanting body?'

'I am no more your beautiful water sprite than I am your sweet Aphrodite,' Desirée snapped. 'And I would thank you to refrain from addressing me in such ridiculous terms. I am not one to be moved by such empty words of flattery. Much to your disappointment, I am sure.'

'On the contrary, I am delighted to find a questioning mind behind so beautiful a face.' He paused for a moment to assess this new piece of information. 'But perhaps I was wrong to try to tempt you with the promise of pretty jewels and fine clothes. Perhaps I should have mentioned the abundance of fine museums and libraries which are to be found in London, all of which are filled with books and artefacts from all over the world. I should have piqued your curiosity with the promise of lectures from learned historians, and teased you with talk of political assemblies held in the homes of some of London's most entertaining hostesses, all of which I could make available to you.'

His hands had stilled but his words were evoking a different kind of excitement in Desirée's breast all together. Oh, how she had longed to visit the cultural centres of London; to see the British Museum, and Westminster Abbey where the tombs of the former kings and queens of England were on display for all to see. To view centuries-old sculptures and priceless collections of Greek and Roman artefacts.

And surely the political hostess he referred to was Lady Holland; a woman who was well known for hosting scintillating parties attended by some of

London's most interesting people. Desirée knew that some of the sharpest minds in England took part in the lively discussions to be had at her home, and though Lady Holland might not be deemed quite acceptable to the highest levels of society, she was, nevertheless, a fascinating woman.

'Come, Aphrodite, what do you say?' he whispered persuasively. 'Come live with me and be my love, and we will all the pleasures prove.'

The misuse of the Marlowe poem, originally intended for a passionate shepherd to the lady he wished to court, brought sparks of anger to Desirée's eyes. 'I do not doubt that you expect me to be flattered by your estimable offer, sir, but I am not a simple shepherdess to be so persuaded, nor some willing lightskirt who exists only to pander to your pleasures.'

'Pleasures for us both,' he reminded her smoothly. 'For I assure you, I enjoy both the giving *and* the taking in love.'

It was suddenly too much for Desirée. She was submersed to her neck in a woodland pool, wearing a shift that was as transparent as a fairy's wing, and she was having a conversation with a stranger in the most normal of tones about going to London and becoming his mistress!

Truly, he was no better than the old Marquis of Sywell himself, for he, too, had believed that any girl in the neighbourhood was ripe for the picking.

'I have no desire to become your mistress, sir, nor that of any man,' Desirée said in a voice not unlike that which she had used to chastise Elizabeth Perry earlier in the day. 'I am an intelligent woman and one who thinks too highly of my own worth to debase myself in such a manner. But do not fear. I am sure there are many who would be only too eager to accept your offer. And now, if you will kindly turn your back and allow me a few moments of privacy, I shall be on my way.'

After a moment's hesitation, the man reluctantly inclined his head. 'Very well. Never let it be said that Sebastian Moore would force a lady to do anything she did not wish to. For there must be mutual respect and affection for a liaison to achieve any level of satisfaction—even in one such as this.'

Then, without warning, he bent his head and kissed Desirée full on the mouth. His lips were warm and possessive over hers as his arm closed firmly around her waist and drew her against the long hard length of his body.

'Farewell, Aphrodite,' he murmured against her mouth. 'I shall not soon forget you or our chance encounter here.'

Then the man called Sebastian Moore turned and began to swim back in the direction from whence he had come.

In the quiet of the woodland pool, Desirée stood and gazed after him long after he had disappeared from view. She knew that she should dress and make haste to return to school, but somehow, thoughts of duty and obligation were far from uppermost in her mind. She kept thinking about the way his fingers had brushed ever so lightly against her breast. She had never been touched like that before; never been made to feel as though her body was burning hot yet icy cold at the same time.

Then she thought about the way he had kissed her, remembering how incredibly soft yet firm his mouth had felt against hers. The heat of his lips against the coolness of hers had evoked the strangest feelings of excitement and breathlessness.

But who was this Sebastian Moore whose touch had sparked such a traitorous response from her body? Why did the sound of his voice yet linger in her mind? He had asked her to be his mistress! He had treated her with a complete lack of respect, speaking to her in a way that no gentleman would ever speak to a lady. He had even kissed her—without so much as a by your leave! Surely she should be repulsed by a man who took such liberties, and who clearly thought so little of her as an individual.

Yes, of course she should. And she would go back to Guarding's and laugh about this with Helen. She would tell herself that she was glad she would never have cause to see such a reprehensible gentleman again.

'And maybe in time, I might even come to believe it,' Desirée whispered as she slowly climbed out of the pool and started to dress.

Chapter Two

14 May, 1812

The occasion of Desirée's twenty-fifth birthday was not a cause for celebration. All it signified to Desirée was the passing of another year and one which had been difficult for any number of reasons, not the least of which was Miss Elizabeth Perry—or more specifically her father, Viscount Perry. Desirée had been introduced to Lord Perry at the time of Elizabeth's enrolment at Guarding's, as were all of the teachers to the parents of every new student. On first acquaintance, she had thought him to be a handsome man with pleasant manners and was not surprised when some of the other teachers had professed themselves quite taken with his charm.

But Desirée had soon come to realise that beneath the guise of the gentleman lay a man who was both disreputable and untrustworthy. He seemed to have a knack for appearing in a room when she was in the presence of only the younger girls and more than once she had felt his eyes upon her, only to see him glance away when she turned to look at him.

But lately, he had stopped troubling himself to look away. Now when Desirée looked up, it was to find him watching her with a boldness she found both disconcerting and frightening. For that reason, she had begun taking pains not to be in the same room with him. When she knew that he was visiting Elizabeth—which he seemed to be doing with increasing regularity—Desirée kept to her room. If he arrived prior to the dinner hour, she made sure that she was in the company of one of the other teachers, most often Helen de Coverdale, with whom she finally shared her concerns.

'But *why* will you not speak to Mrs Guarding about it?' Helen whispered as they stood together in Desirée's classroom at the end of the day. 'I am sure she would be most upset if she knew that Lord Perry was making improper advances towards you.'

'But that is just the problem, Helen, he hasn't made any advances towards me yet,' Desirée admitted. 'It is simply the way he *looks* at me. Besides, who is to say that Mrs Guarding would believe me if I were to tell her?'

'Why would she not?'

'She might believe that I was imagining it. Or worse, that I had somehow encouraged his attentions myself.'

Helen glanced at her in astonishment. 'How can you even suggest such a thing, Desirée? You have been here for over six years and in all that time there has never been a whisper of scandal about you. Why do you think Mrs Guarding would suddenly believe that you were encouraging a gentleman's attentions?'

Desirée smiled sadly. 'Perhaps *because* I have been here for six years and there has never been a whisper of scandal about me. Perhaps she thinks that as another birthday approaches, I might decide to cast aside discretion for one reckless taste of impropriety.'

'Tosh, I do not believe that for a moment,' Helen asserted. 'You are a model of propriety, Desirée. You would never do such a thing, and we both know that you have had opportunity to.'

At Helen's words, a memory flashed into Desirée's mind; the memory of a handsome face, a masculine voice, and the most improper suggestion it had whispered. It was a memory which had come to her more than once during the past year, and it was one which—Desirée was embarrassed to admit—had caused her more than a fleeting moment of regret.

Helen was the only person in the world to whom she had confided the details of her meeting with the handsome stranger. And it was from Helen that Desirée had learned that Sebastian Moore was actually Viscount Buckworth, a noted rake and man about town. From her friend, Desirée had learned that Lord Buckworth was a wealthy gentleman with a fine house in London and a large estate in the south of Kent.

But she had also learned that he was a man who enjoyed the company of women. It seemed that he had never been seriously attached to any one woman, but that he had kept a string of beautiful young mistresses, all of whom had enjoyed his generosity both during *and* after their association. And while Helen had been astonished to learn that Lord Buckworth had made Desirée such a proposal, she had been equally practical in her assessment of it.

'It is only natural that your first reaction would have been shock—and that your immediate response would have been to turn it down,' Helen had said at the time. 'After all, we have been raised to believe that marriage is the ultimate goal of any well-bred young woman, and that to be a courtesan is the worst possible thing which could befall us. And yet, I wonder if in truth it would really have been all that bad.'

At Desirée's shocked exclamation, Helen had smiled her lovely smile and lifted her shoulders in a graceful shrug. 'Only think of the freedom you would have enjoyed, Desirée. Especially when compared to the life you live now. You would have had a fine house to live in and servants to attend you. You would have had beautiful clothes and jewels to wear, and you would have been seen on the arm of a handsome and charming gentleman. You would have been able to go to the opera and masquerade balls, and even to the museums and libraries you love so much.'

'But I would have been his…whore!' Desirée had cried, blushing as she had stumbled over the word. 'I would have been forced to…give him my body in exchange for an opulent lifestyle that might end at any time. Indeed, I should think that with a man like Lord Buckworth, the future would be very precarious indeed. He likely changes his mistresses as frequently as he changes his cravat.'

'Ah, but think of the pleasures you would have

enjoyed whilst you were under his protection, Desirée,' Helen had said, surprising Desirée with the note of envy in her voice. 'You would have had the freedom to walk about town during the day, and to visit the pleasure gardens by night. You would have had shops to browse in and amusements to exclaim over. You might even have been able to go riding with him, had he thought to provide you with a suitable mount.'

Desirée had thrown up her hands in despair. 'Yes, but I would have been…a fallen woman, Helen. A creature despised by society.'

'And are we as teachers thought of so very highly by society now?'

The question had stopped Desirée dead. She hadn't had an answer then, nor did she have one now. It had been an extremely disturbing revelation to say the least.

'Speaking of your birthday—' Helen said softly now, 'I have something for you.' She dug into a hidden pocket in her gown and pulled out a small box. 'Happy birthday, dear Desirée.'

Desirée looked down at the gift in Helen's hand and felt her eyes fill with tears. 'Oh, Helen, there was no need—'

'Of course there was,' Helen whispered. 'But it is not so very much. Just a little something I made for you, so there is no need to cry. Oh dear, and there is the bell for dinner.'

Desirée sighed. When Mrs Guarding rang the bell, woe betide anyone who did not heed its calling. But because of the time she and Helen had spent talking, there was not enough time for her to go up to her room and safely tuck her present away. Nor had she pockets in her gown like Helen.

'Why don't you put it in the slate cupboard?' Helen suggested. 'You can always come back for it after dinner.'

'Yes, of course,' Desirée said with relief. 'No one will be likely to look for it there.'

So saying, she carefully tucked the precious box at the back of the cupboard and closed the door. 'Thank you, Helen. I really do not know what I should do without you!'

Dinner at the Guarding Academy for Girls was not the unpalatable meal so often to be had at English boarding schools. In fact, Mrs Guarding prided herself on the quality and the variety of food served at the Academy. She was often heard to say that a body starved was a mind starved, and if there was one thing the headmistress demanded from her girls, it was the constant use of their brains. Fortunately, she employed a cook who was somewhat feared by the local tradespeople, and who had, on more than one occasion, taken a supplier to task for trying to sell her inferior goods.

Dinner that night, for example, consisted of a savoury chicken pie, served with bread and boiled potatoes, followed by custard and fruit. The girls sat at two long wooden tables with one teacher sitting at the head, and one at the foot. Conversation was not forbidden, but it was to be kept to a polite level. Mrs Guarding appeared at the beginning of the evening meal to lead them in grace, and if she was not otherwise engaged, generally sat down to eat with them. If she did retire to her private dining-room, it usually meant that she was entertaining a visitor, either a local person of some importance, or one of the girls' parents.

Mrs Guarding had retired to her dining-room tonight, but Desirée had no need to guess at the identity of the visitor. She had already seen Lord Perry's carriage in the courtyard and knew that after dining with Mrs Guarding, he would spend some time with Elizabeth before heading back to Town.

Desirée's own relationship with Elizabeth had not improved during the past year. In fact, the girl seemed to have made it her mission to make Desirée's life as miserable as possible. She continued to disrupt the class whenever possible, and was disrespectful almost to the point of rudeness. Of course, Desirée knew that *she* would be the one made to suffer if she did lose her temper, and for that reason alone she endeavoured to ignore Miss Perry's outbursts and to carry on with the class. But it did not make for amiable working conditions, nor for a congenial relationship.

At the conclusion of the meal, the girls rose and quietly left the tables. Desirée rose too, intending to head directly back to her room, when she suddenly remembered the gift Helen had given her. She hesitated for a moment, wondering where Lord Perry might be, and then realised that he must still be with Mrs Guarding. The headmistress usually made a point of being there to bid the girls a good evening. The fact that she had been absent tonight meant that she must still be entertaining her guest—which left the way clear for Desirée to return to her classroom.

Desirée seldom went back to her room after dark. The wing was totally removed from the rest of the school, situated as it was at the far end of the building, and although she had never been one given to flights of fancy, neither did she relish being alone in the deserted corridors. Even now, her footsteps made a hollow, empty sound on the wooden floor. And apart from the eerie glow of the full moon and the rather feeble light cast by her candle, Desirée was surrounded by the night.

She was heartily relieved when she finally reached her room. Opening the door, she hesitated for a moment in the doorway. She knew the layout of the desks and where the cupboard was located, but it felt strange to be moving around in total darkness. She held the candle aloft and carefully moved forward.

She finally found the cupboard she was looking for, and setting the candle on the corner of the desk, Desirée bent down to open it. She put her hand inside and began to feel around for the small box she had secreted there. It was then she heard the words, spoken in a low, lazy drawl, that frightened her far more than darkened rooms and empty shadows ever could.

'Good evening, Desirée.'

Desirée froze, her pulse beginning to beat an erratic rhythm in her chest. Lord Perry! He must have followed her here from the dining-room. But she had not heard his footsteps. Which meant that he had trailed her stealthily, not wishing her—or anyone else—to know.

Desirée rose slowly, forcing herself to remain calm. 'Good evening, Lord Perry.'

He was standing just inside the doorway, the light from the candle in his hand shedding a soft glow on his handsome face. 'What a pleasant surprise to find you here all alone, Desirée. I have been hoping to do so for some time now.'

Desirée only just managed to repress a shiver. Even in the dim light, she recognised the look in his eyes. 'I cannot imagine why, my lord.'

'Can you not?' His mouth curled upwards in a mocking smile. 'I thought that would have been quite obvious to you by now.'

A chill, black silence surrounded them. 'I think it would be best if you were to leave, Lord Perry,' Desirée said quietly. 'It is not seemly that we be alone together.'

'But I have waited so long for just such an occasion, my dear. Surely you would not deprive me of a few moments of conversation now that we are here.'

A weak flutter of hope arose in her breast. 'Do you wish to speak to me about Elizabeth?'

'Elizabeth? Good God, no. I have quite enough conversation with my daughter as it is. She is an impertinent child at the best of times. But then, I am sure I have no need of telling you that.'

Desirée swallowed tightly. 'My lord?'

'Oh, come, Miss Nash, you need not mince words with me. Elizabeth is a cold little bitch who probably enjoys making your life hell. You can blame her mother for that. She raised her in her own image.'

The cold, impersonal manner with which he spoke

of his wife and daughter did nothing to endear him to Desirée. 'Then what would you wish to speak to me about, if not Elizabeth's progress?'

He took a step forward and closed the door behind him. 'I wish to speak to you, Desirée. About the possibility of our achieving…a much warmer relationship than the one we have now.'

A shudder rippled through Desirée's body. 'We do not have a relationship.'

'That is precisely my point.'

Icy fear twisted around Desirée's heart. She had not mistaken the look in Lord Perry's eye. He had followed her down here with one purpose in mind, and unless she did something to prevent it, he was going to attempt to force himself on her right here in the darkness of the deserted classroom.

In spite of her fear, Desirée felt anger and loathing rise in her breast. What right had he to think he could treat her in such a manner! Did he think that because she was a woman and a teacher that she had no feelings? How dare he treat her with such a blatant lack of respect?

Desirée glanced quickly about the room, peering into the darkness for a possible means of escape. Had there been more light, she might have been able to make a dash for the door, but in the darkness, she knew she was likely to stumble over a chair or fall upon a table. Besides which, Lord Perry stood between her and the door. Which left her only one alternative.

'I shall scream,' Desirée threatened in a low voice. 'I swear if you touch me—'

'Oh, I do intend to touch you,' Lord Perry whispered. 'But I do not think you will scream. Because I know that in the deepest recesses of your heart, you don't really want to fight me, Desirée.'

'My name is Miss Nash.'

'Oh yes, I've seen that look in your eyes, Desirée. And I know what it means.'

'Stay away from me!'

'They won't believe you if you say you fought me,' Lord Perry murmured as he took another step closer and set his candle on the desk. 'They'll believe that you encouraged my advances. And why would you not? I can make your life very pleasant, Desirée. I'm a very wealthy man. I can give you anything you ask for. But if you fight me—'

It happened so fast that Desirée had no time to prepare herself. Lord Perry covered the ground between them in a single stride. He reached for the bodice of her gown and ripped it open.

'No!'

'I will have you,' he ground out, his voice thick with desire as he locked his hand around her waist and pulled her against him. 'Come, let me taste the sweetness of your lips.'

Incensed beyond reason, Desirée began to fight. She twisted and writhed in his arms, trying to strike him as she fought to get away, but she was no match for his strength.

'Yes, my little hellcat, a fight only adds to the pleasure,' Lord Perry breathed darkly. 'But I won't have you mark me.'

Pushing her backwards, he pinned her body against

the wall and captured both of her hands in one of his. Shoving them behind her back, he held them there in a punishing grip while his free hand moved aside the fabric of her blouse. 'Beautiful,' he murmured huskily. 'So…beautiful.'

For Desirée, time ceased to have any kind of meaning. She had never felt so humiliated, so utterly degraded, in her entire life. She felt Lord Perry's mouth on her throat and shuddered in revulsion. But when she felt him begin to fumble with the fastenings of his breeches, she opened her mouth to scream, only to have the sound swallowed by his mouth as it hungrily fastened on hers.

Then, from somewhere in the dim recesses of her mind, she heard the sound of the door opening…

'Miss…Nash!'

The shocked and horrified voice of the headmistress reverberated around the dark room like a clap of thunder. As Lord Perry took his mouth from hers, Desirée turned in horror to stare at the cluster of women who were gathered in the doorway. A group which included Mrs Guarding and Helen de Coverdale, and behind them, Elizabeth Perry and Isabel Hewton.

'It would seem that we have been discovered, my dear,' Lord Perry observed, seemingly unconcerned by the interruption. With no outward show of haste, he let go of Desirée's hands and stepped away from her. 'I told you that your room would have been a more appropriate place for a rendezvous, but you would not wait.'

Desirée choked back a cry as shock drained the

blood from her face. 'How can you suggest—I never said—'

'Miss Nash, attend to your clothing!' Mrs Guarding interrupted sharply. 'I will speak to you later.' She turned to the two young girls behind her. 'Back to your rooms, both of you!'

Reluctantly, the girls scampered away. Desirée raised her hands to the torn bodice of her gown as the gravity of her situation began to sink in. 'Mrs Guarding, please—'

'Lord Perry, if you would be so good as to wait for me in my office,' Mrs Guarding said tonelessly.

Straightening the folds of his cravat, Lord Perry offered them a thin smile. 'I am, of course, at your service.' Then, as a final humiliation, he turned back to Desirée and bowed. 'Your servant, Miss Nash.'

Desirée closed her eyes in disgust. She turned away from Lord Perry and prayed that she would not be physically ill.

As soon as the man left, Mrs Guarding breathed a heavy sigh. 'Go to your room, Miss Nash,' she said quietly. 'I will expect you in my sitting-room in half an hour. Kindly do not be late.'

'Mrs Guarding—'

'Miss de Coverdale, be so good as to assist Miss Nash.'

It was clear from the tone of the headmistress's voice that she would brook no argument, and Desirée hung her head in shame. She could only imagine how this must look. She had been caught in a darkened room, locked in a passionate embrace with the father of one of her students. It would not matter that it had been nothing short of an attempted rape. Because he was a nobleman, and she a teacher, there would be no quarter given. She alone would be held up for blame and censure.

Worse, the fact that the episode had been witnessed by two of the Academy girls made any hope of salvation impossible. Desirée knew how Elizabeth Perry would make it sound in front of the rest of the school. Her reputation would be in shreds.

Her life at Guarding's was over.

Desirée felt the softness of a shawl being draped around her shoulders, and looked up to see tears shimmering in Helen's eyes. 'Are you all right?' Helen asked, looking decidedly shaken by the night's tragic events.

Desirée nodded but her eyes were haunted. 'It wasn't what it seemed,' she whispered wretchedly.

'On the contrary, Desirée, it was *exactly* what it seemed,' Hélen said. 'But I fear that is not how it will be made out to be. Come, my dear, we must get you ready to see Mrs Guarding.'

The interview conducted in the privacy of Mrs Guarding's sitting-room proceeded much as Desirée had expected it would. It was evident from the way the older woman spoke that she was deeply regretful of the circumstances which had precipitated the meeting, but nevertheless, the conclusion was inescapable.

'I am very sorry to have to do this, Miss Nash,' she said quietly, 'but under the circumstances, I have no choice but to dismiss you.'

Sitting on the faded chintz sofa across from her,

Desirée raised her eyes to the level of the headmistress's. 'But I did not encourage Lord Perry's advances, Mrs Guarding. Please, you must believe me. I had…gone back to my classroom after dinner to collect a birthday present Miss de Coverdale had given me. He—Lord Perry—must have followed me. I did not hear his footsteps, but when I turned around, he was standing in the doorway. On my honour, I *swear* that is what happened.'

Mrs Guarding sighed, but it seemed to Desirée, a heavy sound filled with regret. 'Whether you are guilty or not does not signify, Miss Nash. What does, is that you were caught in an extremely compromising position by myself, another teacher, and two of our students.'

'One of whom is a young lady who makes no secret of the fact that she has no affection for me,' Desirée pointed out.

'I cannot deny that that is so, Miss Nash. But surely you can see that because of the rancour which exists between you and Miss Perry, what happened tonight will be used to destroy you.'

The words rang like a death knell in Desirée's head. 'Is there nothing I can say to convince you?'

Mrs Guarding rose slowly to her feet. She was a handsome woman still, her youthful beauty having been mellowed by the passage of the years. But her eyes were as sharp and as discerning as they had ever been. 'I am afraid there is nothing that anyone can say,' she said regretfully. 'Lord Perry's character is not unlike that of many of his peers. And as much as I might resent it, the word of a woman against a man such as that counts for little in this world. Young ladies will gossip, Miss Nash, and therein lies our problem. I do not expect for one minute that Elizabeth or Isabel will keep this to themselves, and once word gets back—as it inevitably will—to the parents of the other girls, questions will be raised and fingers will most certainly be pointed. For me to keep you here now would be to condone what happened.' Mrs Guarding paused. 'I have to think of the reputation of the school, my dear. I hope you can understand that. I have been longer in this world than you, and I know how unkind people can be. News of this will get about soon enough, and I have no doubt that it will be embellished and enhanced until it will rival the goings-on up at the Abbey.'

'Mrs Guarding,' Desirée began desperately, 'the last six years have been very special to me. To have had an opportunity to work with educated and intelligent women like yourself, and to try to foster that knowledge in other young women, has been more fulfilling than anything else I might have done with my life.'

Mrs Guarding nodded, and in the soft light of the candles, the grey strands in her hair glowed like silver. 'And you have been an excellent teacher, Miss Nash, which makes this all the more difficult for me to do. But I hope that under the circumstances you can understand why your tenure here must end. And why I cannot provide you with a reference.'

Desirée clasped her hands together in her lap to keep them from trembling. No, she could not understand. She could not understand or accept that the six years she had been a teacher here suddenly counted for nothing. That in the blink of an eye, her reputation and her future had been ruined by the thoughtless actions of an arrogant man.

'Have you anywhere to go, Miss Nash?' Mrs Guarding asked quietly. 'Any family with whom you can find a home until you manage to secure other employment?'

Like one awaking from a dream, Desirée slowly looked up at the headmistress and shook her head. 'No. There is…no one.'

Mrs Guarding sighed. 'I feared that might be the case. That is why I always like to keep a little aside for emergencies.' Turning towards the sideboard, the headmistress removed a small key from the ring at her waist and opened the bottom drawer. From within, she drew out a small velvet pouch and placed it in Desirée's hand. 'It is not a lot, but it should help tide you over. And I do not expect you to pay it back.'

Desirée glanced down at the bag in the palm of her hand, and felt her eyes fill with tears. There was so much she wanted to say, and yet, what could she say that would make any difference?

'You have been…more than kind, Mrs Guarding,' she said at last. 'Thank you.'

Then, knowing that it was time, she got up and turned to go.

'Miss Nash,' the older woman said abruptly, 'you are welcome to stay for a few days while you make enquiries into a new position.'

Desirée managed a feeble smile. 'Thank you, Mrs Guarding, but I think it is best that I leave as soon as possible. Word of this will get out soon enough and as you say, you have the reputation of the school to consider. And…while I know it won't change anything now, I do want you to know that…what happened tonight truly was not my fault.'

Sadness glowed in the warm blue eyes that looked back at her. 'If it is of any consolation at all, Miss Nash, I never believed that it was.'

In her tiny room on the top floor of the building, many things went through Desirée's mind that night, not the least of which were the extremely dim prospects for her immediate future. She had been dismissed in disgrace. Turned off without a reference. And without a reference, she could not hope to approach a reputable school or a respectable family for work. Even as a governess she would be expected to provide a letter from her past employer. The problem was, Mrs Guarding was the only employer Desirée had ever had, and she was coming away from her with nothing.

Stifling a groan, Desirée rolled over on to her back and stared up at the ceiling. What would it be like to leave Mrs Guarding's after all these years? This tiny room had become her home, and Mrs Guarding and the staff her friends and family. All of them had played an important part in her life. A part which, as of tonight, had come to an abrupt end.

So what were her choices now? Desirée's thoughts turned briefly to the likelihood of employment in the immediate area. There were several shops in Abbot Quincey, along with the post office and the coaching inn. And while she had no desire to work as a tavern maid at the Angel, perhaps she might apply to Mrs Hammond for a position in either the general store or the linen-drapers. Or even to Mr Westcott at the bakery.

But close on the heels of that came the realisation that she would be no more likely to find a job in the village than she would anywhere else. Word would soon spread that Miss Desirée Nash had been found in a compromising position with the father of one of her students, and what respectable doors would be opened to her then?

All right, then what other options did that leave her? Where would her tarnished reputation not work against her? Desirée thought hard for a moment. She might be able to get a job on one of the farms. There was always plenty of work to be had, and farmers generally didn't ask too many questions as long as the work was done. Nor was Desirée afraid of hard work. But she was afraid of the tedium her days would offer. She would find no intellectual companionship among the loutish farm lads, nor with the young maids who tended the goats or milked the cows. And if she ended up working in the kitchens, she would be at the beck and call of the cook or the housekeeper, both of which could make her existence a nightmare.

Her prospects were looking very dim indeed.

The answer finally came to Desirée about an hour later—and it was an indication of her state of mind that she did not dismiss it out of hand. In truth, it shocked her so very much that she abruptly got out of bed and began to pace back and forth the confines of her room.

Desirée Nash become a *courtesan*?

No, it was quite impossible, she assured herself. It was…too ridiculous for words. She could never lower herself to such an unseemly and disgraceful existence. Indeed, the very thought of it made her shudder, as it would any educated, well-brought-up young lady.

No, there had to be another way. All she had to do was think of it.

Unfortunately, as hard as Desirée put herself to think of an alternative, nothing came to mind. For every good idea she came up with, logic provided twice as many reasons as to why it would not work. But there had to be something she could do. Something other than…throwing herself into the protection of a man who was not her husband—and was never likely to be. But what? She had lost both her reputation and her good name as a result of being found in Lord Perry's embrace tonight.

But that was an accident, a little voice whispered in her head. *A mistake. You know the truth of it and so does Mrs Guarding.*

Yes, she did, Desirée reflected grimly, but what did her own opinion and that of a school headmistress count for in the overall scheme of things? When word of this got out, society would draw its own conclusions as to her conduct, and she doubted they would be kind. Added to which was the undeniable fact that, should Lord Perry be questioned about his part in the proceedings, he would certainly deny any charges of guilt. He would be the first to proclaim that Desirée had lured him to her classroom, and that she had been perfectly amenable to a tumble…until they had been discovered, at which time she had cried foul. Was that not what he had claimed this very evening when Mrs Guarding had questioned him about the matter?

As the first light of dawn stretched its golden fingers across the sky, Desirée made her decision. Crossing to her writing table, she pulled forth paper and ink and sat down to write the letter that would, if accepted, change the course of her life. She did not think too hard or too long about the content or the words, for she knew that if she did, she would surely change her mind. But when the missive was done and dispatched, she returned to her room, sat down upon her bed and closed her eyes in despair.

The deed was done. She could not change her mind now, even if she wanted to.

The response came three days later. The letter, scrawled in a bold, masculine hand on heavy cream vellum, was delivered personally into Desirée's hands by a liveried servant, and the content of it was mercifully brief and to the point.

It informed her that the gentleman in question would be pleased to take the young lady on in the capacity suggested, and that if she could arrange transportation as far as Bredington, he would endeavour to take care of the rest. It was signed with one word.

Buckworth.

Chapter Three

Sebastian Moore stood at ease in front of the long window in the study at Bredington. His hands were clasped lightly behind his back and his posture was relaxed as he surveyed the wooded hills beyond. The hunting-lodge had long been a favourite retreat of his. It belonged to his good friend, George Lyford, Viscount Wyndham, a gentleman whom Sebastian had first encountered at Angelo's Haymarket Room where he regularly went to practise his fencing skills. Although a good deal younger than Sebastian, Wyndham had proved himself a worthy adversary, and the two had soon become friends.

It was Wyndham who had first invited Sebastian to join him for a weekend at the remote country lodge. And ever ready for an excuse to get out of London, Sebastian had accepted with alacrity, knowing that Bredington offered some of the finest shooting and fishing in the land. And hidden as it was in the rich forests around Steepwood Abbey, it offered peace and tranquillity from the frenetic pace of London.

Now, as Sebastian gazed at the woodlands surrounding the lodge, he thought about his reasons for being at Bredington today, and about the meeting he was soon to have. How strange to think that, as a result of a casual swim in the river last summer, he was this very day to acquire a new mistress.

The thought brought a smile of expectation to Sebastian's face, just as it had the day the unusual letter had arrived at his townhouse in London. In fact, he'd had to read it twice before fully comprehending that the lady—who had identified herself only as Miss Nash, and their meeting by a geographical point of reference in her letter—was asking if the offer the gentleman had made to a certain young lady in July of last year was still in good standing?

It had taken only a moment for Sebastian to recall the occasion and even less for him to remember the young woman. The image of her rising out of the water to stand in a bright patch of sunlight, with her arms stretched out towards the sun and her glorious body clad in nothing but a sodden chemise, had lingered in his mind for a very long time. But never in his wildest dreams had he expected to hear from her again.

The fact that the lady had made no reference to *his* name—which Sebastian knew he had given her—lent an element of subterfuge to the correspondence, and had led him to believe that she was not willing to risk discovery. For that reason, he had likewise made no reference to anything in his response, except by the application of his title, which would hardly condemn him if the letter were to fall into the wrong hands. But Sebastian had no concerns that it would. He had given it to one of his own servants with the instructions that it was to be taken to the address the lady had specified in her letter and that it was to be put into none but the lady's own hands.

And very soon, she would be here. He had instructed her to meet him at Bredington, and to arrive early enough in the day that they could set off in time to reach London by nightfall. That way, he would be able to settle her in the house he had rented for her, and possibly to commence their relationship forthwith.

Sebastian smiled in anticipation of the coming night. Yes, it made for a most pleasing prospect altogether.

Desirée had taken a quiet leave of Guarding's. She had said her goodbyes to Helen and Mrs Guarding the night before, knowing that it would be easier than at the actual time of departure. The following morning, she had waited until the girls were at class before slipping out through the back door to the waiting chaise. Now, as she travelled along the road she knew so well, she began to wonder what lay in store for her.

She had refused to think too long or too hard about the upcoming meeting with Lord Buckworth. Indeed, she found that if she thought about it for more than a few minutes, her palms began to grow damp and her heart to beat in a most alarming manner. But she knew that she could not back down. By sending her letter to Lord Buckworth, she had set her course. With his acceptance, she had committed herself to it.

The only bright spot in the proceedings was that since receiving his letter, Desirée had taken her plan one step further. If nothing else, agreeing to become Lord Buckworth's mistress would provide her with a means for getting to London. And once she was there, she intended to look around for alternate employment. She knew there were agencies in London that handled that type of thing.

The main thing now was to get to London as expediently as possible. Thanks to Mrs Guarding, she had a little extra money to look after expenses, but there was no question in her mind that travelling to London with Lord Buckworth would provide the most economical and comfortable way of doing so.

Desirée suffered a brief stab of conscience at the thought of misleading the man, but then decided that her sympathies were surely misplaced. After all, *he* was the one who had mistaken her for a woman of loose morals in the first place. To her mind, providing her with a means of getting to London was the very *least* he could do in the way of an apology!

In all too short a time, Desirée found herself following a liveried manservant through the panelled corridors of Bredington. Eventually he opened the door to a room which appeared to be a study. He then bowed towards the gentleman who was standing by the window watching her. 'Miss Nash, my lord.'

'Thank you, Manson. Have the carriage brought round and readied for departure. We leave within the half hour.'

'Very good, my lord.' The servant bowed and withdrew, leaving Desirée alone with the man she had encountered in such a humiliating way all those months ago.

'I am surprised you told him your name. Your letter led me to believe that discretion was of the utmost importance.'

Desirée inclined her head. 'Had the servant been connected to one of the local families hereabouts, I would not have vouchsafed it, even now.'

'So you are confident that he is not?'

'I know most of the families in the villages,' Desirée replied, 'and I know which sons and daughters work at the big houses. Your man has the look of a gentleman's valet, not of a household servant.'

Sebastian Moore leaned back against the edge of his desk and crossed his arms over his chest. 'Your assessment is quite correct, Miss Nash. Manson has been with me for some time and has travelled with me from London.'

Desirée again inclined her head and allowed herself a few minutes to study the man standing opposite. He had changed little since the occasion of their first meeting. He was every bit as large and as intimidating as she remembered. In the polished Hessians, he stood well over six feet and his long legs were clad in buckskins that fitted like a second skin. His beautifully tailored jacket had been made to accommodate the width of his massive shoulders and although the musculature of his chest was hidden now behind a silk shirt and cravat of impeccable whiteness, Desirée remembered how it had looked with a wet shirt clinging to its every ripple.

His face, too, was as she remembered it. Handsome enough to make any young girl's heart beat faster, but with a devil-may-care look in his eyes that warned anxious mamas to be wary. His lips were full and sensuous, his mouth curving upwards in a disturbing smile.

Desirée sighed. He was all that she remembered. His ease of manner and the quality of his clothes proclaimed him for the gentleman she'd known him to be. And despite the fact that this was their second meeting, she felt more than ever that she was standing in the presence of a complete stranger.

'Am I as you remembered, Aphrodite?'

The familiar term of endearment brought a flood of embarrassed colour to Desirée's cheeks. 'To be honest, I find that I remember…very little of our first encounter, Lord Buckworth,' she lied, hoping that it sounded more convincing to his ears that it did to hers. 'But I am moved to comment that you do look somewhat…different with your clothes on.'

His smile broadened and turned sensual. 'As do you, my dear, for I have carried the memory of what you looked like with your clothes *off* close to my heart since last July.'

The comment was meant to put her off stride—and it did. 'A gentleman would not remind a lady that he had seen her…*en déshabille*,' Desirée said, struggling to recover her composure.

'And as I told you last year, Miss Nash, I am no gentleman. That has not changed.'

Desirée was grateful that he did not repeat the other

assertion he had made last year. Namely, that *she* was not a lady.

'But never mind that,' Sebastian continued. 'I think it is time that we made some proper introductions. And in the absence of anyone to do it for us, I shall take the liberty of doing it myself. I am, as I think you already know, Sebastian Moore, Viscount Buckworth. And you are…?'

Desirée took a deep breath and clasped her reticule a little tighter. 'Miss Desirée Nash.'

She saw his eyes widen in amusement. 'Desirée. From the Latin, *Desirata*. She who is desired.' A devilish look came into his eyes. 'How appropriate.'

His knowledge of Latin took her completely by surprise, and in spite of herself, Desirée smiled. 'Sebastian. From the Greek, *Sebestyen*. To be…revered.' Her eyes took on a decided sparkle of their own. 'How decidedly less so.'

'Oh-ho! I think that I shall have to mind my words around you, Miss Nash. At least until I have found out, and can use to my advantage, some of your own…weaknesses.'

There was a distinctly sensual undertone to his words, and it served to remind Desirée of the reason she was here. For all their bandying about of words, Lord Buckworth was not looking at her as a social or intellectual equal. He was looking at her as the woman who would soon warm his bed. 'Lord Buckworth, I—'

'Sebastian.'

Desirée stared at him in dismay. 'My lord, our acquaintance is not—'

'Of the kind that makes it necessary for us to engage in formal language,' Sebastian interrupted smoothly. 'At least, not in the intimacy of our chambers…Desirée.'

Her name was the softest whisper on his lips, and the words Desirée had been about to utter completely deserted her. Oh yes, he certainly had a way with women. He had likely only to speak their names in that honeyed way to have them melt into his waiting arms. Well, she did not intend to melt. In fact, as soon as she got to London, she was going to…

Abruptly, Desirée stopped. She was not going to be doing anything for herself when she got to London. Because the moment she did, she would be occupied with duties of a different kind entirely. She had applied to this man for his protection. And liking what he had seen in the forest all those months ago, he had agreed to take her to London and to establish her there as his mistress.

As soon as she got to London, *that* was what she was going to be doing.

Desirée hung her head, fighting back a wave of shame and embarrassment. Dear Lord, what had she done? What had she sentenced herself to? She could not even take pleasure from the fact that Lord Buckworth had remembered her, or that his response to her query had come so swiftly. Indeed, she almost wished now that he had retained no memory of her at all and that she had been left to find some other means of employment. At least as a servant she might have aspired to some level of dignity. What had she left of any worth now?

'Your carriage awaits, my dear,' Sebastian asked softly. 'Shall we go?'

Desirée could not meet his eyes. She was heartsick at being unable to think of an answer to her dilemma. Truly, she was no better off here than she had been at the pool last summer. For just as he had there, Sebastian Moore had the advantage of her here as well.

The first half hour of their journey passed in silence. Desirée kept her face turned towards the window as they drove the half mile to the tiny hamlet of Steep Ride, and then on to Abbot Giles. In her heart, she bid a silent farewell to the countryside that was as familiar to her as her own name. They passed by the church where Mr Hartwell delivered his sermons every Sunday, and then past the tiny cottage where Lucinda Beattie, the former vicar's spinster sister lived.

Desirée knew them all. She had met them at Lady Perceval's annual summer fête, held on the grounds of Perceval Hall. It was one of the few times in the year when everyone from servant to master met to play games and enjoy the day—even teachers from Mrs Guarding's Academy. From there they passed through the southern tip of Giles Wood before connecting with the road which, three miles on, would put them on the main Northampton to London road. From there, it was on to London and her new home.

As if sensing her need for time, Sebastian did not press her for conversation. He seemed content to let her stare through the window, letting her thoughts take her where they would. But she knew that in the closed confines of the carriage he watched her. She could feel his eyes on her, inspecting every inch of her appearance from the tip of her light brown hair to the toes of her serviceable brown boots.

Finally, as they left the Abbey villages behind, Desirée drew a long, deep breath. Her past was precisely that now. Something she was leaving behind in the dust raised by the carriage wheels.

'You claimed there was nothing holding you to the area,' Sebastian said quietly, 'and yet, I cannot help but remark on the regret and unhappiness I see in your face at leaving it, Desirée.'

His comment was perceptive, and the tone in which he offered it surprisingly gentle. Desirée sighed and drew her eyes away from the window. 'When one has lived and worked in a place for so many years, my lord, one develops a certain attachment to it, even if it is only for the comfort of the routine it has provided.'

'Are you fond of routine?'

'I am comfortable with it,' she repeated. 'There is a difference.'

'Yes, I suppose there is. But as a woman who would cast off her clothes and swim in the river, you do not strike me as the type who would be comfortable with routine.'

A fierce blush suffused Desirée's cheeks. 'I hope you do not intend to keep reminding me of that occasion at every opportunity, my lord?'

Sebastian smiled at her irritation. 'Not at every opportunity, no. But it did leave a lasting impression upon my mind.'

Desirée studiously avoided his gaze.

'You mentioned that you worked in the area,' he commented as the silence lengthened again. 'What manner of employment did you leave?'

Desirée's first inclination was to remain silent. After all, what need was there for him to know anything about her past life or what she had done in it?

'I am not trying to pry, Desirée,' he said, as if reading her thoughts. 'But the hours will pass more quickly if we endeavour to fill them with amiable conversation. Or at least with the exchange of useful information.'

Realising that it served no useful purpose to prevaricate, Desirée took another deep breath and raised her eyes to his. 'I was…a teacher at Mrs Guarding's Academy for Girls.'

He smiled his mercurial smile. 'A teacher?'

'Yes. Of Latin, Greek, and philosophy.'

This time he stared at her in astonishment. 'Good Lord, it would seem that I have indeed taken up the company of a bluestocking.'

Desirée blushed. The term was not generally flattering, but it was hard to tell from Sebastian's tone what his true feelings on the subject were. 'Does that bother you?' she asked, almost hoping to hear him say that it would.

Unfortunately, it seemed that she was mistaken in her assessment of him.

'Surprised? Yes. Bothered? On the contrary, it will

no doubt provide us with ample subjects upon which to converse when we are not otherwise engaged.'

His meaning was perfectly clear, and once again, Desirée felt her cheeks grow warm. Heavens, would she never be able to stop blushing in the man's presence?

'Mrs Guarding's Academy has a reputation for being somewhat forward-thinking, as I recall,' Sebastian said conversationally. 'Did you enjoy being a teacher there?'

It was Desirée's turn to be surprised. She had not expected a London rake to be familiar with the reputation of a country school, no matter how illustrious some might consider it to be. 'I always enjoyed the subjects I taught,' she said carefully, 'perhaps more than I enjoyed the teaching of them.'

'I take that to mean that not all of your students were as anxious to receive instruction in the ancient languages and philosophies as you were to provide it?' he ventured.

Despite her feelings of awkwardness, Desirée was able to dredge up a smile. 'Most of them were. In fact, I believe that some of the girls asked to be sent to Guarding's *because* of the opportunity it allowed them to study subjects which most other girls' schools viewed as strictly male-oriented. The philosophies of Aristotle, for example, are not generally discussed among ladies of a certain social class.'

'Pity,' Sebastian observed. 'It might make for more enjoyable time spent in their company if they were.'

Desirée flicked him a look of surprise. 'You are familiar with the teachings of Aristotle?'

'Not as familiar as you, perhaps, but I am acquainted with some of his more common precepts. But tell me, Miss Desirée Nash,' Sebastian said, 'if you enjoyed being a teacher at Mrs Guarding's excellent academy and were comfortable with the routine it provided, why did you apply to me?'

Desirée hesitated. She had prepared herself for this question. Anticipated it, in fact. But now that she had been asked and was faced with having to tell him an outright lie, she found that the words of deception would not come so easily to her lips.

'I felt the need for a…change in my life,' she said, stumbling a little over the words. 'I wanted to see something of the world, and I could not imagine doing that from the confines of a girls' school.'

He regarded her in silence for a moment with those piercing blue eyes. 'So you applied to a man you had met on the bank of a river and asked him if he would take you on as his mistress.'

His words were blunt and Desirée had no doubt he meant them to be. But it was too late to change her story now. 'I saw in your offer a chance to…broaden my horizons,' she replied softly.

Thankfully, this time his reply came in the form of a throaty chuckle. 'Well, it's been called many things, Desirée, but I doubt it's ever been called an opportunity to broaden one's horizons.' His eyes caught and held hers. 'So there was no reason other than this sudden lust for adventure which prompted your writing a letter to me and asking me to take you to London as my mistress.'

Again, Desirée flinched. She wished she could

think of something else to say, but there was nothing. Besides, what was the point in telling him the truth? Would he think any better of her for having been told that she had been caught in a compromising position with one of the girl's fathers? More importantly, would he believe her?

Of course he wouldn't—why should he? He had seen nothing in her behaviour thus far to lead him to believe that she was a fine upstanding young woman. He had already accused her of being less than a lady by swimming half-naked in a public place. Now she was sitting in his carriage on the way to London to become his mistress. What kind of credibility did that lend her?

'Desirée?' he prompted.

'I told you…I was simply looking for a change,' Desirée repeated stubbornly. 'Is it so out of the realm of possibility to think that a five-and-twenty-year-old spinster might wish to have a change at this time in her life?'

The bitterness in her voice astonished her—as did the fact that hot tears of dismay were welling up in her eyes. What did this fine London gentleman know of humiliation? What manner of social injustice had the lofty Viscount Buckworth ever been forced to endure? Certainly nothing that would have induced him to turn his back on everything he knew to cast himself into the path of destruction.

Desirée quickly averted her face, blinking hard to keep the hot tears from disgracing her—and then caught her breath when she felt the warmth of Sebastian's large hand on her arm.

'No one is forcing you to do this, Desirée,' he said in his deep, quiet voice. 'You have only to say the word and I shall turn the carriage around and take you back to Steep Abbot. I have no wish to force myself upon you. But when I received your letter, I thought it was your desire to become my mistress. If that is not the case, tell me now and let that be an end to it. No wrong has been committed and I will not be offended. And I am sure Mrs Guarding will be happy to take you back. After all, how many young ladies with a background in Greek, Latin and philosophy is she likely to have encountered within the space of a few days?'

The sentiments, which were expressly intended to offer her comfort, were the last things Desirée expected from Lord Buckworth. She had not expected compassion or understanding from a man who was well known to be a rake and womanizer. He was giving her an opportunity to turn around; to go back before her reputation was well and truly lost.

And for a moment, just for a moment, she was tempted to do it. But what had she to gain by it? What possible good could be achieved by her returning to Mrs Guarding's Academy now?

Sadly, the question provided its own answer.

'My lord—'

'Sebastian.'

Desirée offered him a faint smile. 'Sebastian. It is…very good of you to be so…understanding of my circumstances and I thank you for your consideration. But I…do not wish to change my mind. I have made my decision and I must stand by it.'

Besides, it was already too late, Desirée reminded herself. She could not turn back now even if she wanted to. The damage to her reputation had already been done. Lord Perry had seen to that. The gates to her past were closed and locked.

Sebastian sat back against the squabs and studied her. 'All human actions have one or more of these seven causes,' he recited quietly. 'Chance, nature, compulsion, habit, reason, passion, desire.'

Desirée smiled. 'Aristotle knew much of men and their actions, but it was Sophocles who said, fortune is not on the side of the faint-hearted.'

'So you go to London to seek your fortune, Miss Desirée Nash?' Sebastian enquired.

'I go to London to seek my *future*.' Desirée met his gaze straight on. 'Only time will tell what manner of fortune it holds.'

They stopped for lunch at a roadside inn. Sebastian secured a private room in which they might dine, and while it was a pleasant enough place, it was there Desirée experienced first-hand what life as Sebastian's mistress would be like—both the good and the bad of it.

To the good, Sebastian was a perfect gentleman. He was kind and attentive to her needs, and ensured that she had everything she required. But while her clothing was respectable, the fact that she was travelling with a gentleman who was clearly a member of the aristocracy, and that she did so without benefit of a maid or chaperone, proclaimed her to be either a family member or his mistress.

Had she been a better actress, Desirée might have been able to convince those around her that she was indeed, Sebastian's sister or niece. Unfortunately, the lack of ease with which she moved in his company soon put paid to those circumstances. And judging by the way the innkeeper and his wife kept looking at her, and then at each other, Desirée knew that they had made their own assessment of the situation.

She was exceedingly grateful when they got on the road again.

Thankfully, the weather was clement and they made good time. Sebastian dozed for an hour or so in the afternoon, allowing Desirée to relax a little and enjoy the passing scenery. It had been a long time since she had travelled through this part of the country, and it was exciting to see how, or if, it had changed. But in truth, Desirée did not find the countryside nearly as interesting as the man who was sitting across from her.

For the first time, she was able to take a good look at this man with whom her immediate future was now irrevocably entwined. She observed that his hair was not black as she had first thought, but a very dark shade of brown into which a few stray streaks of grey had found their way. His eyelashes were surprisingly long and of the same dark shade as his hair and brows. In sleep, his face was as relaxed as that of a child. Desirée found herself able to admire the shape of his wide brow and the fine, aristocratic nose.

His fingers were laced together across his chest and he had unbuttoned his jacket for greater comfort. Yes, his clothes would certainly proclaim him for the gentleman that he was, Desirée acknowledged. His Hessians shone with a gleam indicative of an attentive valet, and the superb manner in which his clothes fitted his large body gave evidence of a tailor worthy of his craft. But beneath all the trappings of wealth and class, what was this man called Sebastian Moore really like?

As was his habit, Sebastian woke quickly, rising from the depths of slumber to instant consciousness. His eyes snapped open and he found the soft green eyes of his companion fixed upon him. Seconds later, he saw the colour rise to her cheeks—and watched her eyes dart quickly away. 'Too late, Aphrodite,' he murmured in a throaty voice. 'I caught you looking. Do you approve of what you see?'

'You are…mistaken, my lord,' Desirée assured him hastily. 'I merely…chanced to look in your direction as your eyes were opening. I was actually engaged in a study of the scenery beyond.'

Smiling, Sebastian drew himself into a sitting position and stretched. 'You know, there is something which has been niggling at me ever since I received your note. A bit of information which I would like to have clarified.'

Desirée glanced at him warily. 'What information is that?'

'Just before we parted last summer, I told you that my name was Sebastian Moore. At the time, you evidenced no knowledge as to who I was and I assumed that you would have no reason to. And yet, the letter I received in London was addressed to Sebastian Moore, Viscount Buckworth. How did you learn of my identity? And this time, I will have the truth, Desirée,' Sebastian warned her. 'You do not have the face to lie. Your pretty green eyes give you away.'

A dark shadow of lashes dropped down over those enchanting eyes, but a few moments later when they lifted again, Sebastian could see that they were clear. 'Well?'

'One of the teachers at the Academy…knew who you were,' Desirée said hesitantly.

'Good Lord. You actually *spoke* of our interlude to someone at the school? You continue to surprise me, Desirée.'

'I only told her because I knew that I could trust her implicitly,' Desirée explained in her own defence. 'When I explained what had happened and…mentioned your name, Helen told me who you were.'

'I see. And was it…Helen's idea that you apply to me for protection?'

Desirée gasped. 'Certainly not! The idea was mine and mine alone.'

'I'm glad to hear it. But what else did she tell you about me, other than my title?'

By the blush which appeared in Desirée's cheeks, Sebastian knew that it must have been quite a lot. 'Ah, let me guess.'

'My lord, I—'

'No, please, Desirée, you would be amazed at how good I have become at this. Let me see. She probably would have started off by saying that Viscount Buckworth is a gentleman of good family, not to be found lacking in either money or property, but that he has, upon numerous occasions, shown himself to be something of a rake and a ne'er-do-well,' he recited thoughtfully. 'He likes to gamble, both at cards and at horses, and has been known to lose a fortune in a single night's sitting—only to claim it all back again through a fortunate turn in luck the next.'

'Lord Buckworth—'

'No, wait, there is more,' Sebastian continued cheerfully. 'I have no doubt that my reputation with the fair sex precedes me. So I must assume that you are aware that I play with the affections of many of the young ladies who are presented to me, but that I continue in my bachelor ways and find pleasure instead with a string of beautiful young mistresses.' He glanced at her quickly to gauge her reaction. 'I see I have the right of it.'

'Well, yes, you do, more or less.'

'Was there anything I left out?'

'No, not really.'

'You are not being truthful with me, Aphrodite.'

Desirée fidgeted in her seat. 'It is...not the type of thing to be discussed—'

'Ah, but it is, my dear. Because there is nothing that we cannot discuss together, and I should like to know what advice she gave you. Did she tell you that I was a drunk and a reprobate—'

'Of course not.'

'Or that I was foolhardy and reckless—'

'Not at all!'

'Perhaps she intimated that I was a cruel beast with a vicious temper who beat my mistresses on a regular basis?'

Desirée uttered another gasp. 'She said nothing of the kind! In fact, she told me that you treat your mistresses with the utmost kindness, and that you continue to do so even after you have—' She broke off in dismay, her eyes wide. 'Oh, dear! I never should have said—that is, I didn't mean to suggest—why are you laughing?'

'Why am I laughing? Dear me, I should have thought *that* would have been very obvious,' Sebastian said when his laughter finally subsided. 'Your friend obviously had a good source of information indeed. Even I was not aware that I was possessed of such benevolence of spirit. Is that why you wrote to me, Aphrodite? Because you knew that if I agreed to offer you my protection, I would treat you well, both during our liaison and afterwards?'

Desirée opened her mouth to speak and then abruptly closed it again. How could she tell him that he was her last resort? That she had applied to him because she had no other choice?

Her silence was its own response. 'Well, you shall soon have opportunity to see if they are right,' Sebastian said softly. 'For as of tonight, you shall have a comfortable house in which to live, beautiful clothes in which to dress, and a big, soft bed in which to express your pleasure and gratitude. Not a bad way, I think, to start…how did you put it? Broadening your horizons?'

Chapter Four

The house that Sebastian had chosen for Desirée was of modest though pleasing proportions and was located in a discreet though respectable area of town.

Sebastian was looking forward to reaching it. He was anxious to see Desirée settled, and then to return home to his own bed. He had no intention of spending the night with her. As anxious as he was to see her lovely young body again, he knew there was more to the young woman's story than she was telling him, and he sensed she needed some time alone to work things out in her mind.

Sebastian had been totally in earnest when he had asked her if she wished to back out of their arrangement. He had never forced a woman in his life, and he certainly had no intention of starting now. But when she had declined, albeit with some hesitation, he had concluded that the part she was not telling him counted for a good deal. She was obviously of good though not high birth, and had been educated in more than just the ancient languages. So it was only natural for him to conclude that the life upon which Desirée had embarked would be as alien to her as it would be to any other well-brought-up young lady.

For that reason, it occurred to Sebastian that if she would not tell him details of her most recent life, perhaps he could encourage her to speak of her earlier one.

'When were you last in London, Desirée?' he asked as they reached the outskirts of the metropolis.

Desirée had been eagerly glancing out of the carriage window, but at his question, a shutter dropped down over her eyes. 'A very long time ago, sir. I was born in London, but we...moved to the country when I was very young. My parents occasionally brought me back to visit relatives, but that was all.'

Sebastian glanced at her quickly, surprised to hear that she had any relatives in London at all. 'Do you still see these relations?'

Desirée shook her head. 'No. My grandfather was very angry when my mother went against his wishes and married my father. He told her that...she was marrying beneath herself and that if she went ahead with the marriage he would have nothing more to do with her.'

'And she went ahead with it?'

'Of course. My parents were in love,' Desirée said, as if that explained everything.

Sebastian smiled at her naïveté. 'I see. And your grandfather never forgave her?'

'Never. Even when I wrote to tell him of her passing, he did not reply. Nor did he come to her funeral.' Desirée glanced at him earnestly. 'Could you imagine not attending your own child's funeral, my lord?'

Sebastian shrugged. 'No, but then such things seldom do to people who are not of such a nature, Desirée. Your grandfather may have thought that he was acting in your mother's best interests by forbidding her to marry a man whom he perceived to be unworthy of her.'

'But how could he not have seen how much in love they were?' Desirée cried. 'Surely a father would wish to see his only daughter married to someone she loved, rather than to someone she did not, even if he was possessed of a title or a great fortune.'

'Perhaps her father was hoping that by providing her with one, she might, in time, come to feel the other. It is not unheard of for love to develop within the confines of an arranged marriage.'

Desirée sighed. 'I know, but for all that, I could never find it in my heart to feel charitable towards him. He came to see me when I was very young and he frowned at me the entire time. I thought him quite dreadful.'

'I daresay you would,' Sebastian said, hiding a smile. 'Have you any desire to see your grandfather now?'

'The possibility no longer exists,' Desirée said regretfully. 'I received a letter from his solicitor last year, informing me that Sir George Owens had died and that I had been left nothing.'

'I beg your pardon!' Sebastian glanced at her in shock. 'Did you say…Sir George Owens was your *grandfather*?'

'Yes, why? Did you know him?'

'I certainly knew *of* him,' Sebastian muttered, not

adding that what he had known of the crusty old termagant would not have endeared him to anyone. Good Lord, what a cock up this was turning out to be. It was bad enough finding out that his beautiful water nymph was an erudite young lady who taught Latin and Greek at a well-known girls' school. But to discover that Miss Desirée Nash from Steep Abbot was also the granddaughter of the late Sir George Bartholomew Owens cast an entirely different light on the situation.

How could he possibly make a baronet's granddaughter his mistress?

Close on the heels of that dilemma came another. Namely, if he wasn't going to make her his mistress, and she had no desire to return to Steep Abbot, what in God's name *was* he to do with her?

Sebastian thought hard for a moment, thankful that their destination was still some miles off. He had no intention of taking her to the house on Green Street now, but where else *could* he take her? Not to his own home, that went without saying. And if he put her at an hotel, there was a distinct possibility that someone might see them together and begin to ask questions. So where—

And then the answer came to him. Of course! Why hadn't he thought of it before? Aunt Hannah would help him. She had done so more than once in the past.

Sebastian thumped his cane on the roof of the carriage and instructed the driver to take them to an address in Mayfair.

The abrupt change had Desirée glancing at him in

alarm. 'Are we not going to our original destination, my lord?'

'No. I suddenly remembered that…repairs are still being carried out in one of the rooms upstairs,' Sebastian told her. 'I had forgotten about that when I gave John the directions. I think it best that you stay with my aunt until the house is ready for occupation.'

Mistaking his hesitation at having had his plans disrupted for annoyance, Desirée nodded. In truth, she was relieved at having been spared—if only for a night or two—the reality of entering her new life. But the idea of having to stay with Sebastian's aunt was not an entirely comforting prospect either. The lady would no doubt be a pattern card of propriety and one easily able to discern the nature of the relationship which existed between her nephew and the young woman travelling with him.

After all, she reflected grimly, well-to-do gentlemen simply did not bring single, unattended ladies to London with them for any purpose—but one.

On first appearance, Sebastian's aunt was everything Desirée had expected her to be. A handsome rather than pretty woman, Hannah, Lady Charlton looked to be in her mid to late forties and conducted herself with all the grace and dignity of her position. Her hair was a rich, dark brown, elegantly styled, and her face was smooth and unlined. She was quite tall for a woman, standing a good head taller than Desirée, but her height lent her an elegance and stature that a shorter woman could never hope to achieve.

'Sebastian, what a delightful surprise,' Lady

Charlton said when her nephew and his guest had been shown into the comfortable drawing-room. 'I was only thinking the other day that I had not seen you this age. How are you, my dear?'

'Very well, thank you, Aunt,' Sebastian said. He smiled as he bent forward to kiss her cheek. 'I hope you will forgive my stopping by so late—'

'My dear, you know that you need never make apologies to me.' Lady Charlton's bright blue eyes flickered towards the young lady who was standing quietly in the background. 'But come, will you not introduce me to your companion?'

'Aunt Hannah, may I present Miss Desirée Nash. Desirée, my aunt, Lady Charlton.'

Silently drawing a breath, Desirée stepped forward and gracefully curtseyed. 'My lady.'

'Desirée. What an unusual name. From the French, is it not?' Lady Charlton asked, glancing at her nephew.

Sebastian shrugged his shoulders in a charmingly cavalier fashion. 'I thought it was Latin.'

'Well, never mind, it is uncommon to say the least.' Lady Charlton looked at Desirée and did not even attempt to disguise her curiosity. 'How do you and my nephew come to be acquainted, Miss Nash?'

'Actually—' Sebastian began.

'I asked Miss Nash the question, Sebastian,' Lady Charlton said pleasantly. 'Can she not speak for herself?'

'Lord Buckworth and I met in the vicinity of Steep Abbot, my lady,' Desirée said quickly. 'The small village where I was living.'

'Yes. We were both enjoying the pleasures of a warm summer's day,' Sebastian piped up.

'Really. And dare I ask *how* you were enjoying the pleasures of the day?'

Aware that Sebastian had phrased his answer poorly, Desirée hastened to explain. 'We were swimming, my lady.'

'*Swimming?*'

'Yes. In the River Steep.'

'Good gracious! Not in public view, I hope?'

'On the contrary, the pool was located deep within the forest and was very private,' Desirée assured her.

To her credit, Sebastian's aunt evidenced little of the shock she must have been feeling at the news. 'I see.' She turned to direct an amused glance at her nephew. 'And how did you happen to be in the area of a private pool in the woods near Steep Abbot, Sebastian?'

'I was staying with Wyndham at Bredington for a few days and decided to go for a swim.' Sebastian's smile flashed briefly. 'Purely by chance, I happened to arrive at the pool the same time as Miss Nash did.'

'And the two of you swam in it…together?'

The word conveyed a wealth of meaning and brought a hot flush of embarrassment to Desirée's cheeks. 'Y-yes, my lady, but only for a very brief time. I was not aware of…Lord Buckworth's presence when I first arrived. I have never encountered anyone in the glade before, and was astonished and alarmed when I discovered that I was not alone.'

'You may not have been aware of *his* presence, Miss Nash, but I find it difficult to believe that my nephew was not aware of *yours*,' Lady Charlton drawled.

'Lord Buckworth informed me that he was asleep when I arrived, ma'am, and that he was not aware of my presence until my splashing woke him. He left shortly thereafter.' Desirée did not intend to tell her of the argument which had ensued before Sebastian had reluctantly agreed to leave.

'I see.'

Desirée felt the lady's eyes upon her and knew that she was assessing everything about her, from the colour of her hair to the unstylish cut of her clothes. She wished that Sebastian would say something, but he seemed content merely to watch the two ladies study each other. Finally, Lady Charlton walked back towards the bellpull and said in a voice that gave no indication as to her feelings, 'Have you dined, Sebastian?'

'Not since lunch, Aunt Hannah.'

'Good. Then you would not object to partaking of some light refreshment?'

Sebastian inclined his head. 'I'm sure we would both be most grateful for the opportunity.'

The door opened shortly to admit the butler. 'Yes, my lady?'

'Grant, would you be so kind as to ask Cook to prepare a light supper for my nephew and his guest. Then perhaps you would show Miss Nash to the Green Room. I think she might like to freshen up before dinner.'

Desirée glanced at Lady Charlton in surprise. 'Thank you, Lady Charlton, I would indeed.'

'Travelling is a dusty occupation, but a necessary one,' Lady Charlton observed kindly. 'Grant will show you the way.'

Desirée inclined her head and followed the ramrod-straight figure of the butler from the room.

Lady Charlton waited for the door to close behind them before turning an inquisitive eye on her nephew. 'Now, Sebastian, would you care to explain what all this is all about—and tell me why you have brought your mistress to my house?'

Sebastian winced. For all her grace and refinement, his aunt could be painfully blunt when she chose to be. 'Desirée is not precisely my mistress.'

'Then what precisely is she?'

He thought for a moment, wondering whether it would be judicious to temper truth with fiction, or whether he should just blurt it all out. He decided on the latter. He had learned long ago that when dealing with his aunt, honesty was always the best policy.

'Miss Nash is a young woman I was bringing to London to *become* my mistress, but one who, on the way here, disclosed certain facts to me which made me think better of my decision.'

Lady Charlton's eyebrows rose. 'Indeed. I think that before the young lady returns, Sebastian, you had best tell me all about Miss Nash. Brandy?'

'Yes, thank you.' Sebastian waited while his aunt filled two glasses and then handed one to him. That was yet another of the things he loved about her. She did not adhere to the custom of polite social drinking at the prescribed times. When she wanted a brandy, she had one. But then, Hannah Charlton had long been considered something of an Original.

'Miss Nash is, or rather was, a teacher at a private girls' school in the village of Steep Abbot,' Sebastian began. 'We met, as she said, one afternoon last summer when she had slipped away to enjoy a swim in the River Steep. I had swum up from Bredington and was taking a brief respite on the bank, well hidden from view, when Miss Nash appeared out of the woods and started to undress.'

Lady Charlton smiled. 'So you were not asleep?'

He offered her a sheepish grin. 'No. I merely said that in an effort to allay her feelings of embarrassment. But I did wait until she had enjoyed her swim and had climbed back out on the bank again before making her aware of my presence.'

'How gracious of you, Sebastian,' came the laconic reply. 'I will spare us both the embarrassment of asking you if the young lady was wearing any manner of clothing—'

'As a matter of fact, she was—'

'By asking you how you came to discover that she was a teacher.'

'Actually, that was one of the things I learned today.' Sebastian had the grace to look contrite. 'At the time, I was not particularly interested in what Miss Nash did for a living.'

Lady Charlton shook her head. 'Really, Sebastian. You saw a beautiful young woman and immediately dismissed her intellectual standing to think only about her potential as your bed partner. How typical of you and your sex. So, Miss Nash was employed as a teacher. Where?'

'At Mrs Guarding's Academy for Girls in Steep Abbot.'

'Mrs Guarding?' Lady Charlton stared at him in shock. 'Good Lord, could that be…Eleanor Guarding?'

'I have no idea, Aunt. I did not think to delve into the identity of the headmistress either.'

'What subjects did Miss Nash give instruction in?'

'Greek, Latin, and philosophy.'

Lady Charlton began to smile. 'Then it would have to be Eleanor Guarding's school. I am aware of no other establishment that would offer such advanced subjects to women.'

'Are you acquainted with the venerable Mrs Guarding?' Sebastian asked, not even attempting to conceal his surprise.

'Not acquainted, but certainly familiar. I chanced to read one of her papers a few years ago. It gave a rather chilling depiction of female slavery and its effect upon society as a whole.' Lady Charlton glanced at her nephew shrewdly. 'As a teacher at Mrs Guarding's Academy, Miss Nash is not your usual type of ladybird, Sebastian.'

'No, that much I discovered today, Aunt,' he agreed ruefully. 'But that is nothing compared to what I learned about her as we were arriving on the outskirts of town.'

Lady Charlton gazed at him expectantly. 'Well?'

'Miss Desirée Nash is the estranged granddaughter of the late Sir George Owens. What do you think of that?'

The look of astonishment on Lady Charlton's face told him exactly what she thought, and more. 'Good heavens, that comes as something of a shock indeed. I knew that Sir George had one daughter and that he had disowned her as a result of her marrying a man of whom he did not approve. But I had not heard news of a child resulting from that union.'

'Well, one did,' Sebastian told her. 'And once I realised what Miss Nash's connections were, I could not, in all good conscience, set her up as my mistress. Word travels too fast in this town and I could only imagine what Sir George's family would say if they were to discover that I had taken his only grand-daughter as my *fille de joie*.'

Lady Charlton laughed softly. 'Yes, I have no doubt that such a diverting piece of news would make its way around town very quickly indeed.' She studied her nephew's handsome face in silence for a moment. 'So, what do you intend to do now? Take Miss Nash back to Steep Abbot?'

Sebastian sighed and stood up in a gracefully rest-less motion. 'I can't. I gave her the option of returning to Steep Abbot today and she told me that she could not.'

'Could not, or did not wish to?'

'She led me to believe that she did not wish to, but I tend to think there is more to it than that.'

Lady Charlton rose and poured herself another glass of brandy. 'I am quite sure there is, Sebastian. I have trouble believing that a well-born young lady who gave instruction in the ancient languages and philosophy, and who was accepted by a woman like Eleanor Guarding, would suddenly decide to turn her life upside down and become a courtesan. Tell me, what exactly did Miss Nash say her reasons for coming to London with you were?'

'She said that she felt it was time for a change in her life,' Sebastian said, repeating the words he himself had spent considerable time reviewing on the way here. 'When I said that it was *quite* a change, she informed me, rather bluntly, that at five-and-twenty, she had every right to do so.'

'Sebastian, did you *ask* this young lady to become your mistress?'

'No. Well, that is to say, not *recently*. I did allude to the idea last summer when I met her, but at the time, Desirée told me exactly what she thought of my suggestion. So you can imagine my surprise when I received a letter from her just last week, addressed to me here in London and asking me if the offer I extended to her last summer was still open. I wrote back saying that it was…and here we are.'

Lady Charlton nodded thoughtfully. 'Well, I suspect you are right about one thing, my dear. There is certainly more to Miss Nash's story than the little she has shared with you. For an educated young woman to do what she has done is unthinkable. I can only conclude that something desperate must have happened to her to bring about this astonishing change.'

'I tend to agree, Aunt Hannah, but the question remains, what I am to do with her now? I feel responsible for having brought her here, but I cannot in all good conscience set her up in the house on Green Street,' Sebastian said quietly. 'The news will surely get back to Sir George's family and I am just as like to be called out as to be left to go about my business.'

Lady Charlton nodded. 'Yes. Families can be funny things. Sir George might have disowned his daughter and ignored his grandchild, but there is nothing to say that his heir will not suddenly feel his responsibilities. Especially when he learns that a not so distant family member is now the mistress of a man whom Sir George referred to on more than one occasion as a rakehell and scoundrel.'

Sebastian tossed back the rest of his brandy. 'Yes, I am well aware of what Sir George's feelings about me were.'

There was a moment of silence as they both contemplated the situation.

'Look, why don't you leave Miss Nash here with me for a few days?' Lady Charlton offered unexpectedly.

Sebastian glanced at his aunt with hope. 'Are you sure?'

'Why not? I have no plans to go out of town, and she seems a pleasant enough young woman. And to be honest, I would welcome the opportunity of talking to someone who has more than dress patterns and gossip on her mind. I have not had occasion to enjoy a good philosophical discussion in some time. I think I would enjoy it.'

Impulsively, Sebastian bent down and kissed her cheek. 'You are a godsend, Aunt Hannah. If you would agree to keep Miss Nash here for a few days,

I can spend the time trying to find her suitable employment elsewhere. In fact, Jeremy and Regina Stewart have just had another child, and their eldest daughter is now five. Perhaps they would consider employing Miss Nash as a governess.'

'It is worth a try, Sebastian, but that is not to say that Miss Nash will welcome the opportunity.' Lady Charlton's eyes sparkled. 'If I had the choice of becoming the mistress of one of London's most handsome and eligible bachelors, or governess to a five-year-old child, I wonder which I should choose.'

Sebastian threw back his head and laughed. 'Dear Aunt Hannah. I should like to think that as my aunt, you would do what was socially and morally correct. However, *because* you are my aunt, I tend to think you would do the other and say to hell with what everyone thought.'

'Pray do not tell our young guest that.' Rising to her feet, Lady Charlton tucked her hand in her nephew's arm and winked at him. 'I should like to retain some pretence of dignity for a little while at least!'

For Desirée, Lady Charlton's suggestion that she freshen up before dinner had been a most welcome one. The trip had been long and emotionally draining, and notwithstanding the comfort of Sebastian's carriage, Desirée was weary. She was also extremely apprehensive about going back downstairs and facing Lady Charlton again. She knew that the lady suspected the nature of her relationship with Sebastian.

To believe otherwise was to pretend an ignorance of the most simple of facts.

Respectable unmarried ladies simply did not arrive with single gentlemen, unescorted and unattended, in the early hours of the evening. And knowing that, Desirée could not help but wonder what opinion the lady had taken of her. She knew that during her brief absence the situation would have been made clear, so it was quite likely that Lady Charlton would refuse to allow her to take a meal with them, let alone stay in her home for a few days!

It was that certainty which accounted for the shock Desirée felt when, upon re-entering the drawing room, she discovered that not only was she to stay for a meal and for the night, but that she was to remain at the house as Lady Charlton's guest for a few days.

'But…I don't understand,' Desirée said with a confused glance at Sebastian.

'It is really quite simple, Miss Nash,' Lady Charlton said. 'My nephew has explained that the establishment in which you were to reside is in need of repairs. That being the case, I have offered to put you up here until they are finished.'

'That is…most kind of you, Lady Charlton, but given the circumstances of my being here, I would understand perfectly if you did not wish me to stay. I am sure I could find lodgings elsewhere.'

'There is no need for you to go elsewhere, Miss Nash,' Lady Charlton assured her. 'I have plenty of room, and as I was telling Sebastian, I am looking forward to the opportunity of engaging in conversation with an educated young woman. I understand that you were employed as a teacher at Mrs Guarding's Academy for Girls?'

Desirée blushed, certain now that the conversation during her absence had been about her. 'Yes, I was.'

'Eleanor Guarding is a remarkable woman,' Lady Charlton commented. 'Would that more gentlemen paid heed to her teachings. If they did, I feel certain that the cause of women would be greatly improved.'

'You are acquainted with Mrs Guarding, my lady?' Desirée asked in surprise.

'Not personally, I regret to say, but I am very familiar with her work. What woman of intellect could not be?'

Inordinately pleased that Sebastian's aunt was in sympathy with Mrs Guarding's philosophies, Desirée felt some of her apprehension ease. 'She is a remarkable woman indeed, Lady Charlton, and the school is a reflection of all that she is. I consider myself extremely fortunate to have had the benefit of her employ for the past six years.'

Desirée would have said more, but the drawing-room door opened and the butler announced that a light collation had been laid in the dining-room.

'Splendid. We shall continue our conversation there.'

'*We?*' Sebastian enquired in amusement. 'But surely you have already eaten, Aunt?'

'Of course I have, Sebastian, but I am eager to talk to Miss Nash about Mrs Guarding's school and to learn what it was like to be a teacher there.'

At that, Desirée only just managed to keep the smile on her face. She was pleased that Lady Charlton was familiar with the school and with the formidable woman who ran it. Nor was she surprised that she would wish to know more about what went on within its walls. But as to how she had come to be a teacher there, Desirée knew that if she answered that question, it would only be a matter of time before Lady Charlton asked her why she had left it.

And that troubled her sorely. For while she had been able to fool Sebastian as to her reasons for leaving, she was not at all sure that she would be able to do as convincing a job on Lady Charlton.

To Desirée's relief, there was no inquisition over dinner. Rather, the meal—which consisted of a delicious consommé, followed by slices of cold ham, a selection of cheeses and a creamy custard for sweet—provided an excellent opportunity for Lady Charlton to discuss Mrs Guarding's beliefs in general, and to ask how she had incorporated them into the running of the school.

The subject of Desirée's life there and why she had left did not arise at all.

Desirée also enjoyed watching the exchange of conversation between Sebastian and his aunt. It was clear that a great depth of feeling and respect existed between the two. Their shared laughter over people and events known only to them evidenced a like sense of humour and Desirée could see that they were completely at ease with one another. It brought home to her how much she missed her own family, and the comfort of being with people she loved.

'You look tired, Miss Nash,' Lady Charlton said suddenly. 'Would you perhaps like to retire?'

Desirée touched the fine linen napkin to her lips. 'Thank you, Lady Charlton. I admit, I am weary. It has been…a long day.'

'Yes, and a rather momentous one, I should think. Sleep well.'

As Desirée rose, Sebastian did, too. 'I shall call to see you in the morning. Good night, Desirée.'

Desirée felt the colour rise to her cheeks. For a little while this evening, she had been able to forget that the reason she had come to London was to become this man's mistress. Until she saw the look in Lord Buckworth's eye. Then the memory of it all came rushing back. But to be fair, Desirée knew that she could no longer reproach Sebastian for the direction her life was taking. The gentleman had been kindness itself. He had offered her a graceful escape from her promise and when she had turned him down, he had tried to make the rest of her day as comfortable as possible.

Truly, if there was any blame to be assumed for the position she now found herself in, Desirée knew at whose door it would have to be laid.

'Good night, Lord Buckworth. And I would like to thank both of you—for the kindnesses you have shown me today.' With that, she walked across the room—very conscious of the two pairs of eyes that followed her—and quietly closed the door. Taking one of the candles that had been left at the bottom of the stairs, she went up to her room and once there, sat down on the bed and gazed at her surroundings.

Certainly the luxurious bedroom was a far cry from her humble lodgings at the Guarding Academy. The walls here were covered in the palest green fabric, with window hangings and bed linens to match. There was a large, comfortable bed, a small mahogany desk and a roomy armoire.

Of course, it was only a temporary accommodation, Desirée reminded herself. The house where she was to stay was currently being repaired. It was only a matter of time before she was ensconced there, and that her role as Sebastian's latest mistress would commence.

Refusing to think about that any longer than she had to, Desirée started to get ready for bed. Someone—possibly Lady Charlton's maid—had already unpacked what few meagre belongings she had brought with her, and had laid out her old cotton nightgown. Desirée frowned when she saw that it was wearing thin in a few places, and wondered if she might take some of Mrs Guarding's money to buy herself a new one.

Then, remembering that it was highly unlikely that she would *need* night-clothes, Desirée buried her face in the well-worn fabric, and quietly began to cry.

Chapter Five

As she had been accustomed to doing at Guarding's, Desirée awoke early. She had passed a restful night, no doubt due to the fact that she had been emotionally drained when she had gone to bed, and had slept without interruption until the first light of dawn had edged over the horizon. She yawned and stretched, and then rising, tiptoed across to the window.

The day was a fine one, with the sun shining brightly from a cloudless blue sky. In the street below, flower-girls and milkmaids were selling their wares, along with the countless other merchants who took to the streets in the early hours of the morning.

Desirée leaned against the windowframe and watched the bustle of activity below her. It was hard to believe that she was actually here in London. It brought home to her how much her life had changed in the course of a single day. But it also impressed upon her how far she had fallen. The young women in the streets below were doing an honest day's work for the money that would keep bread on their tables and a roof over their heads.

What was she going to be doing to earn hers?

Feeling some of her pleasure in the day evaporate, Desirée turned away from the window and walked towards the armoire. Her spirits plummeted even further when she realised that she had only two dresses in which to go downstairs, both of a serviceable grey fabric. Her clothes had been fine at school, where all of the teachers had dressed alike, but here in fashionable London, her drab gowns seemed even drabber by comparison.

Still, they were clean and, unlike her nightgown, they sported no holes. Most importantly, they were hers. She had paid for them with her own hard-earned money. A sobering thought when she realised that within a few days, nothing she owned would be earned in such a way.

Lady Charlton eschewed the popular pastime of staying in bed until noon and was already seated in the breakfast-room when Desirée came down. She looked up from her coffee as Desirée entered and greeted her with a smile. 'Good morning, Miss Nash, did you sleep well?'

'Very well indeed, thank you, Lady Charlton.'

'Splendid. You may help yourself to anything on the sideboard. I shall have Grant bring fresh eggs if you wish. To my mind, eggs are one food which do not improve with standing.'

'Thank you, Lady Charlton, but I am sure I will have no need of anything more than is here,' Desirée said. Indeed, after the good but plain fare she had partaken of at the school, the vast array of silver dishes arranged on the sideboard before her promised a veritable feast.

'Dear me,' Lady Charlton said. 'Is that the manner of dress you wore at school?' At Desirée's reluctant nod, she tutted. 'Well, we shall certainly have to do something about that. It does nothing for your colouring or for your figure.'

Desirée glanced down at the gown and blushed uncomfortably. 'I had thought to order some new clothes when I arrived, but I did not know…what I would need.'

'Well, you will certainly need better than what you have on. I think our first order of business will be to take you to my modiste. Mrs Abernathy does excellent work and her prices are very reasonable. Besides, Sebastian is very particular about a lady's attire, and I am sure you will wish to look nice for him.'

It was the first mention Lady Charlton had made of her role in her nephew's life, and it was more distressful to Desirée than she could have imagined. She dropped her fork onto her plate and winced as it clattered against the fine china. 'Forgive me, Lady Charlton, that was clumsy of me,' she said wretchedly.

Lady Charlton studied her in silence for a moment. 'There is no need to apologise, my dear. I tend to be something of a butter-fingers myself at times.' She hesitated a moment longer and then obviously decided that it was time for plain speaking.

'Miss Nash, I will not try to pretend an ignorance of why you are here. We are both intelligent women, and I see nothing to be gained by indulging in deception. But what I do not understand is *why*. Why would a beautiful and educated young woman like you wish to become a courtesan?'

Desirée did not think it was possible for her to feel any worse, but truly at that moment, she did. 'Lady Charlton, I—I—'

'Please do not dissemble, Miss Nash. Sebastian told me that you wrote to him of your own free will *and* that you refused his offer to return you to Steep Abbot. But judging from what little I have seen, I find it hard to believe that this is truly what you want from life. So I shall ask you here and now. Was this what you meant when you wrote to my nephew and told him that you wanted to…broaden your horizons?'

Desirée raised her eyes to those of her hostess and shook her head. 'Not at all.'

'Then why did you say it? Surely this is not really what you truly wish to become?'

Desirée closed her eyes and felt utterly wretched. 'Of course it isn't. But there were no other options left open to me.'

'Good Lord, child, there are always other options. Becoming a courtesan because you *wish* to is one thing, but becoming one because you perceive there are no other avenues of opportunity—'

'But there were no other avenues, Lady Charlton,' Desirée insisted. 'Please do not ask me to tell you why, but you must believe me when I say that my…choices were exceedingly limited. Had there been anything else that I could have done—'

'You would have done it. Yes, I can see that. But I also see that you are very disturbed about this whole affair and I know in my heart that there must be a reason for it,' Lady Charlton said gently. 'Will you not tell me what happened, my dear?'

The offer was more tempting than Desirée cared to admit, but she knew she had to resist. She barely knew Lady Charlton. And while there was compassion in her eyes now, what would happen once she discovered what had taken place in Steep Abbot on that fateful night? How was Desirée to know that the lady would not misunderstand what had happened, and that she would not lay the blame for Lord Perry's seduction attempts squarely at her door?

'I really would prefer not to discuss it, Lady Charlton,' Desirée said quietly, but firmly. 'You have been...very kind to me, and I am more grateful than I can tell you. But it is best that I say nothing. It can have no bearing on the matter.'

'On the contrary, my dear, it can have a considerable bearing on it. Once you enter into the life you have chosen, there will be nothing anyone will be able to do for you. You will be forever lost to respectable society.'

Desirée gazed at her hostess in despair. 'I am already lost to a portion of it, my lady. This will simply remove me from the rest.'

It was clear from the expression on Lady Charlton's face that she wanted to help. But Desirée also knew there was nothing the lady could do. What she was doing right now by giving her a temporary home was consideration enough.

'Well, I shall not push you for a confidence,' Lady Charlton said finally. 'I know there is a great deal more to this story than you are telling me, and I hate to think that nothing *can* be done about it. But you are not a stupid girl, Miss Nash, nor an impulsive one. I am sure you have given this a great deal of thought and I respect the right of any young woman to make up her own mind. But I want you to know that if you ever feel the need to talk, you have only to ask.' Lady Charlton leaned forward to place her hand over Desirée's. 'I give you my word that nothing you say shall leave the confines of this house, or reach my nephew's ears, if you should not wish it to.'

It was a sincere offer genuinely made, and it touched Desirée deeply. She would not have expected such kindness from a woman who was all but a stranger to her. 'Thank you, Lady Charlton. My gratitude for the compassion you have shown goes beyond what I am able to express in words.'

'Well, never mind,' Lady Charlton said brusquely. 'You're a sweet child and I hate to see you throw your life away. Though I suppose if you have to throw it away, you could do a great deal worse than Sebastian. He's a bit of a rogue but he has a good heart and he would never hurt you, which is more than I can say for some of his acquaintances. Speaking of Sebastian,' she said, pressing the napkin to her mouth, 'he told me to tell you that he would call for you around eleven. I have an appointment at half past ten, so I will not be able to keep you company until he arrives, but please feel free to remain downstairs until he does. If you have nothing else with which to pass your time, there are magazines and a small collection of books in the drawing-room.

Then, this afternoon, I think we shall pay a call on Mrs Abernathy to see about some clothes for you, and perhaps this evening, enjoy a little conversation over dinner.'

'Thank you, Lady Charlton, you are being very kind.'

'Nonsense. To tell the truth, Miss Nash, I'm looking forward to the pleasure of some company for a change. My husband has been gone these twelve years and sometimes I find time grows heavy on my hands.'

Surprised to hear a woman like Lady Charlton admit to feeling lonely, Desirée said softly, 'Have you never thought about remarrying?'

'Oh, the thought crosses my mind every now and then, but the plain truth is, I cannot think of anyone who would have me. I am far too independent for my own good,' Lady Charlton admitted with a chuckle. 'I like being able to come and go as I please, and, since I am wealthy enough to look after myself, I have no need of a man to do it for me. But that is not to say that I would not *enjoy* a gentleman's companionship from time to time. Perhaps to go to the theatre with, or to ride out with on a fine afternoon. Speaking of which, do you ride, Miss Nash?'

'I do, though it has been years since I have had the opportunity to do so.'

'Well then, you may ride my mare whenever you wish. Sebastian is a fine horseman and I am sure he will wish to take you riding in the park. I have a lovely little mare, but I don't get out very often, so

I'm sure she would be glad of the exercise. Now, Miss Nash, eat up. You've a busy day ahead.'

At the conclusion of breakfast, Lady Charlton left to prepare for her outing. Not wishing to return to the solitude of her room, Desirée made her way to the drawing-room, where there were indeed an interesting selection of books and magazines to peruse. Taking one from the top of the pile, she sat down upon the blue velvet settee to wait for Sebastian.

It had been a long time since Desirée had had the opportunity to study any fashion magazines, and as she flipped through the pages of a recent copy of *La Belle Assemblie*, she was alarmed to see how dreadfully out of fashion she was. Indeed, she was so engrossed in her study that she did not even hear Sebastian come in.

'Now, here is something new for Miss Desirée Nash,' he teased softly from the doorway. 'The erudite teacher of Greek, Latin and philosophy at Mrs Guarding's excellent academy studying fashion plates at eleven o'clock in the morning. How terribly decadent.'

Startled, Desirée lifted her eyes from the page— and then started to laugh. 'I fear you have caught me out, my lord. I must confess myself guilty. But I would not be telling a lie if I said it is years since I have had time for such idle pastimes.'

'You refer to the study of fashion as an idle pastime?'

'Of course.' Desirée's eyes twinkled. 'You and I both know that my time would be much better spent reviewing the words of Sophocles, for what is education but the constant learning and re-learning of that which we already know? Seneca was right when he said that diligence is a very great help, even to a mediocre intelligence.'

'Hmm, somehow I doubt you possess a mediocre intelligence, Desirée,' Sebastian observed dryly. 'But we all decide for ourselves what is important. I venture to say that most of your pupils are far more conversant with the pages of the magazine you hold in your hands now than they were with any of Seneca's wisdom.'

Desirée sighed and set the magazine aside. 'I daresay you are right, my lord.' She looked up into his eyes, and then away again. 'Have you been to see…the house?'

'The house?' he repeated blankly.

'Yes. Where we were to have gone…last night.'

'Ah, yes, the house. Actually, no, I haven't,' Sebastian admitted. 'I have been engaged in other pursuits entirely.'

'I see. So you have no idea how long the repairs will take?'

'It is hard to say. Sometimes these things can drag on for weeks.'

'Weeks!'

'You sound alarmed, Desirée. Does the idea of staying here for that length of time bother you? To be honest, I had a feeling you might prefer it.'

'Well, yes, I do. That is to say, your aunt is a most charming lady and I am enjoying her company very much,' Desirée said quickly. 'But in all fairness, I cannot continue to impose upon her. Surely you understand?'

'It is my understanding that she is very pleased to have you. Did she not tell you as much this morning?'

'Yes, but she is a polite and gracious woman. She would hardly be so rude as to ask me to leave.'

'She would if she did not like you,' Sebastian said briefly. 'Aunt Hannah is not one to suffer fools gladly. I have seen her send more than one foppish dandy off with a flea in his ear. But she does get lonely, and I know she is delighted at having someone in the house with whom she can discuss matters of intellectual diversity.'

'But she *knows* why I am here with you, Lord Buckworth,' Desirée said, not so easily convinced. 'And knowing that, how can she feel easy about having me under her roof? Her friends in society will surely begin to wonder. I think it would be best if I were to go to the…place you have chosen for me and live there as best I can until the repairs are finished.'

Seemingly at a loss, Sebastian sighed and sat down on the settee beside her. He had not wished to go into it at length, but since she seemed to be pushing him to move things along, he had no choice. 'Desirée, I may as well tell you, I have been giving… considerable thought to our situation.'

'Our situation?'

'Yes. About that of you becoming my mistress.'

Desirée started. 'But I thought we had already settled the matter.'

'Yes, we had, but given the information I am now in possession of—and which I was not at the time I made my offer—I wonder if you might be interested in employing your services…elsewhere.'

'Elsewhere! Lord Buckworth, I am *not* prepared to go as mistress to anyone else, if that is what you are suggesting!' Desirée cried.

'Good God, that's not what I'm suggesting at all. I was talking about finding you employment of a more respectable nature altogether.'

Desirée blinked. 'You were?'

'Of course. In fact, some very good friends of mine have just had another child, and they are interested in speaking to you about the position of governess to their eldest one, who is now five.'

'A governess?'

'Yes. I think it would be an excellent position for you. I know you would get on very well with the family. Jeremy is a fine fellow, and his wife, Regina, is equally good-tempered. And Mary is possibly the most well mannered five-year-old I have ever had the pleasure of meeting.'

Not wanting him to see her despair, Desirée quickly rose. 'My lord, I thank you for your efforts, but I fear I cannot possibly entertain such an offer.'

'But why not? It is not unlike what you were doing in the past, Desirée,' Sebastian pointed out. 'You will once again have an opportunity to instruct young ladies, albeit not in the areas with which you are most familiar. Given their ages, I doubt they are ready for the complexities of Latin, though they might find Greek mythology amusing.'

Desirée bit her lip in dismay. This was all so very difficult. It would be so much easier if she could just tell Sebastian the truth, for without doing so, how could she tell him that she could not be employed by any honourable people for fear of the scandal that might arise?

'My lord, I cannot, in all good conscience, accept such a position,' she told him regretfully. 'For one thing, I have no letter of reference, and it goes without saying that they will ask for one.'

Sebastian's surprise was genuine. 'Mrs Guarding did not provide you with one?'

Desirée hung her head. 'No.'

'I see.' He was silent for a moment, thinking. 'Well, that should not present a problem. Either myself or my aunt would be willing to vouch for you, and that will be good enough for Jeremy.'

'My lord, I repeat, I am most appreciative of your offer, but I'm afraid I must decline.'

'But why?'

'For reasons that I…cannot make known to you, at this time,' Desirée answered, turning away from him.

His frustration evident, Sebastian walked towards the fireplace. 'Desirée, I find myself at something of a loss here. I am of the opinion that you do not truly wish to become my mistress, and yet when I endeavour to find something else for you to do, you persist in turning it down. Why?'

'Because there is little else I am qualified for—any more.'

Sebastian groaned in exasperation. 'Damn it, woman, you cannot keep throwing out statements like that and not expect me to ask questions.'

'Yes, my lord, I can.' Desirée turned back to face

him. 'I have told you all that you need to know about me, and if I choose to keep certain facts to myself, that is my right. You cannot condemn me for that. But if you have changed your mind and do not wish me to be your mistress, you have only to say so.'

'I beg your pardon?' he said in bewilderment. 'What did I say to make you believe that?'

'The fact that you are looking so hard to find alternate employment for me.'

'The reason I am looking for alternate employment is because you are the granddaughter of the late Sir George Owens,' Sebastian pointed out bluntly. 'It has nothing to do with whether or not I want you to be my mistress. You have family in London. How would it look were we to encounter one of them at the theatre one evening?'

Desirée shrugged her shoulders. 'I have no idea how it would look. I have no reason to believe that any of them would recognize me. I have not been presented to society, so how would they know who I am?'

'Trust me, Desirée, they will know,' Sebastian told her. 'If they are anything like your late grandfather, they will make it their business to.'

'Well, whatever the case, the fact remains that there is really no reason for me to trespass on your aunt's hospitality any longer,' Desirée said quietly. 'And with that in mind, I shall begin to make enquiries into alternate accommodations, and then make my preparations to leave.' She rose and gave him a tremulous smile. 'It goes without saying, of course, that there is really no reason for you and I to have anything further to do with one another. But I did want you to know how…grateful I am for everything you have done.'

'Desirée, please, I wish you would reconsider my offer to place you in the home of my friends,' Sebastian said. 'And if you are adamant that you cannot, then at least tell me what manner of position you *did* have in mind, and I am sure that in time I will be able to find something suitable.'

She glanced up at him and quickly shook her head. 'Thank you, Lord Buckworth, but the answer is still no. You and your aunt have already done far more than was necessary. I think it best if I just say…goodbye and be on my way.'

And Desirée did just that. Before she—or Sebastian—had a chance to change her mind.

After the awkwardness of her meeting with Sebastian, Desirée was forced into an even more embarrassing situation in the afternoon, when Lady Charlton insisted on taking her to see the modiste. Desirée had fully intended to tell Sebastian's aunt of the discussion she had had with her nephew that morning, of course, *and* that she would shortly be leaving her home. But Lady Charlton did not arrive back until shortly before they were ready to leave, and she then spent the entire way there telling Desirée about the new furniture she was having made.

And once they reached the modiste's, of course, it was too late. Mrs Abernathy was at her most attentive from the moment they entered the shop until she quickly ushered them both into the private salon in the back. 'Now, Lady Charlton, how can I be of service to you today?' the woman enquired.

'Miss Nash is the daughter of an old acquaintance of mine, Mrs Abernathy,' Lady Charlton said without preamble. 'Unfortunately, we have not had occasion to see one another since her mother died, but now that she is out of mourning and back in London, I am delighted that she has come to spend some time with me. And naturally, when she expressed a desire to have some new clothes made, I thought of you at once.'

'Well, I think we can make the young lady look very nice indeed, ma'am,' Mrs Abernathy said, obviously satisfied with the young lady's credentials. She studied Desirée's drab outfit for a moment, and then snapped her fingers in a way that had her assistants scurrying in all directions. 'I think an apricot sarsenet would go very nicely with the young lady's complexion, as would an apple-green silk.'

And so Desirée spent the next two hours being measured, fitted, turned and draped with every colour, shade and texture of fabric available. She was not given a single opportunity to speak to Lady Charlton alone, and that in itself caused Desirée great concern. She knew that at the rate the bill for the clothes was mounting, the money Mrs Guarding had so kindly given her would be gone before the day was out.

It was not until they had left the shop with two dresses for immediate use and the rest promised for later in the week, that Desirée finally had an opportunity to express her misgivings.

'Lady Charlton, it was very good of you to say that I was the daughter of a friend, and I am exceedingly grateful for everything you have done. But please, you must cancel the order for the other things. These dresses will be fine, and I do not have enough money to—'

'Do not worry about money, Miss Nash, that is no longer an area with which you need concern yourself,' Lady Charlton told her candidly. 'My nephew will wish to see you well and fashionably attired and he is the one paying the bills now. And you certainly cannot go abroad in London society dressed like a schoolmistress—'

'But that is just it, Lady Charlton,' Desirée interrupted, feeling worse with every word the woman spoke. 'I shall not be going about in society. Lord Buckworth has thought better of his decision and we will not be proceeding with our…relationship. As such, I think it would be best if I were to leave your house at the earliest opportunity.'

'What?' Lady Charlton glanced at her in bewilderment. 'But…when did all this come about?'

'This morning when Lord Buckworth called to see me. He explained his feelings of reluctance with regard to his original plan, and he presented me with the offer of another position,' Desirée told her carefully. 'One as governess to some friends of his.'

'And did you not accept the offer?'

Desirée stared into the distance, seeing neither the bustle of people nor the crowded shops around them.

'I did not, for reasons that I could not explain to him, or to you.'

A thoughtful expression descended on Lady Charlton's face. 'Miss Nash, as I told you this morning, I am well aware that there are things you have not told us. I consider myself to be a very good judge of character and I believe that you left Mrs Guarding's employ for reasons that were disturbing and perhaps even embarrassing to you.'

'Lady Charlton, I—'

'Hear me out, Miss Nash. I can well understand my nephew's reasons for changing his mind about you and the relationship the two of you were to have, and I for one, am glad. I do not think you will be surprised to learn that he and I spoke of you last night, and it was then that he informed me of your connection with the late Sir George Owens. I also knew that Sebastian was going to approach you about the position of governess to Lord Jeremy and his wife and I thought it an excellent idea. But now to hear that you have declined it again leads me to believe that it has something to do with your reasons for leaving Guarding's. Because it is evident that it has nothing to do with looking after children, which I assume you enjoy doing.'

'Yes, I do, Lady Charlton, very much.'

'As I thought. And is it also necessary that you secure employment of some kind in the very near future?'

'Yes, my lady.'

'Very well. In that case, I should like to put forward an offer of my own.' Lady Charlton leaned forward in the carriage and looked straight into Desirée's eyes. 'I wish you to consider allowing me to employ you as my companion.'

Desirée gasped. 'Your *companion*! But, my lady, I could not possibly—'

'Listen to what I have to say before you answer, Miss Nash,' Lady Charlton advised. 'As I told you, my husband has been gone this many years, and as a widow, I have the freedom to move about as I wish. But I have in recent years been feeling the loneliness of my life, and I freely admit that the thought of having a companion has crossed my mind more than once. However, I was not sure what kind of person I wished to employ in that regard. I could not see myself spending time with a silly, missish young woman, or one with little more than a simple education to recommend her,' Lady Charlton said plainly. 'You, however, are neither missish nor stupid. Indeed, I believe your company would provide me with a great deal of satisfaction.'

'Lady Charlton, you do me a great honour, but I could not possibly accept.'

'Why not? I am offering you both a home and a means of employment, Miss Nash. And one which I think would be preferable to becoming either a mistress or a servant. Would you not agree?'

Two spots of colour stood out on Desirée's cheeks. 'Most definitely, my lady.'

'Then why do you hesitate? By accepting my offer,

surely you would have an answer to all of your problems?'

Desirée bit her lip in consternation. The position Lady Charlton was suggesting was something she would dearly love to do, but going about as a companion would expose her to a great many people, including those who might have heard of her past. And she would not risk embarrassing Lady Charlton for all the tea in China!

'Lady Charlton, the offer is a generous one, indeed more so than I can say. But my skills are in teaching young ladies subjects of an educational nature. I have not been taught the niceties of being a companion to an elegant lady of society.'

Lady Charlton snorted. 'Gracious, girl, you have all the training necessary. You were raised by a woman of good birth, were you not?'

Desirée did not even attempt to hide her surprise. 'Yes, I was, but—'

'And your father was…?'

'A clergyman.'

'Then your upbringing is as genteel as it needs to be. I have watched you, Miss Nash. In the very brief time you have been with me, I have observed your manners and have found them to be most pleasing. You conduct yourself with grace and dignity, and you speak well and in a most pleasing manner. I see nothing at all in your behaviour or conduct to preclude you from being a most suitable companion to myself. Or anyone else for that matter.'

'But…what would be the nature of my job?'

Desirée enquired, hardly daring to hope that this might come to pass.

'To accompany me to whatever society outings I choose to attend,' Lady Charlton said. 'To visit whatever shops and places I choose to frequent, and to be at my beck and call when I desire. And I warn you, Miss Nash, I can be very demanding at times.'

Desirée carefully hid her smile. 'You paint an intimidating picture indeed, my lady.'

'I would also expect you to play cards with me and to entertain me on the pianoforte after dinner. I do enjoy music but cannot play a note. Tone deaf, as my father used to say. I would also expect you to converse with me, and to discuss matters which are of interest to us both. Do you think you can do that?'

'I think I probably could, my lady.'

'Good. In return, you will be given room and board, a clothing allowance, and one free afternoon a week. Does that suit?'

'Most adequately, my lady.'

'Good. Oh, and one last thing, Miss Nash. You will not be permitted to question which events I ask you to accompany me to. I will also not allow you to question how I introduce you about in society.'

Desirée hesitated, aware of her first vague stirrings of doubt. 'You are within your rights to ask me to attend whatever manner of entertainments you choose, Lady Charlton, but I hope that if I were to express some…reservations about accompanying you on a particular outing, you would consider my feelings.'

Lady Charlton narrowed her eyes thoughtfully. 'I would be willing to listen, Miss Nash. That is only fair. But the final decision must be mine. Do you agree?'

Desirée thought about it. It was hard to believe that a woman she had met only last night was now offering her both a home and a paying position. And one which, in all honesty, hardly seemed like work at all.

'I think I would have to be a very foolish young woman to refuse such an offer, my lady,' Desirée said quietly. 'Thank you, yes, I would be most grateful to accept.'

'Splendid,' Lady Charlton said with obvious satisfaction. 'Well, now that that is settled, we must work out a few of the details. I think that we shall continue with the story I gave Mrs Abernathy, and which is close enough to the truth that it need not be considered a lie. You are the daughter of a friend of mine, and you are staying with me following the death of your parents and a lengthy sojourn in the country. Your presence and intellect will do the rest. And once you are outfitted in the type of clothes suitable to your station, no one will be any the wiser.'

'But…am I not to wear the clothes of a companion?'

'Yes, such as I believe them to be,' Lady Charlton said. 'I will not have you look like a shabby little wren, Miss Nash. You are too lovely for that. Besides, it will give me great pleasure to dress you. I was never blessed with a daughter of my own, so you will have to do.'

The thought that this great lady would treat her in such a way when she knew perfectly well the reasons for her coming to London in the first place all but brought tears to Desirée's eyes. 'I shall endeavour not to disappoint you, Lady Charlton,' she said quietly.

A smile curved the older woman's lips. 'It never occurred to me that you would, Miss Nash.'

Chapter Six

And so began the next phase of Desirée's life. The house in Mayfair became her permanent home and the charming bedroom on the third floor, her own private domain.

Lady Charlton took her to see Mrs Abernathy again and promptly ordered a whole new wardrobe for her. She justified the expenditure by saying that, as Desirée would be accompanying her on a wide variety of visits and excursions throughout the day, it was imperative that she have the proper type of garments to wear on each and every occasion.

Desirée noticed that Lady Charlton did not cancel any of the lovely evening gowns that were already on order for her, but when she asked about it she was told that she would still need those for the more formal functions the two of them would attend in the evening.

All in all, it helped raise Desirée's confidence immensely. She quickly regained her sense of self-worth, secure in the knowledge that she was once again earning her keep. Certainly it was a much more appealing prospect than being kept by Lord Buckworth, Desirée assured herself.

As to that gentleman, she had seen nothing of him at all since the morning five days ago when they had spoken together in the drawing-room. Perhaps that was why she felt a little nervous as she stood in the hall waiting for Lady Charlton to come down. Sebastian had suggested a carriage ride through the park, and while Desirée was looking forward to it, she could not deny to feeling a considerable degree of apprehension as well. She was no longer his intended mistress, but the companion of his own dear aunt. She wondered how he would feel about her in such a familiar role.

'Ah, Miss Nash, prompt as always,' Lady Charlton said as she descended the staircase a few minutes later. 'Excellent. I deplore tardiness.'

'As do I, my lady,' Desirée informed her with a smile. 'It was one thing Mrs Guarding would not tolerate from either her staff or her students.'

'You must tell me more about Mrs Guarding and her school,' Lady Charlton commented as she pulled on her soft kid leather gloves. 'I am fascinated by her ability to successfully operate an establishment dedicated to the furthering of academic excellence in young women. It is truly a remarkable achievement, and she, a remarkable woman.'

Recalling her conversation with Mrs Guarding on the night of Lord Perry's attack, and the kindness that lady had shown her, Desirée smiled wistfully. 'She is indeed, my lady.'

Soon after, Sebastian arrived at the front door,

looking all the crack in a dark blue jacket over buff-coloured breeches. Desirée had almost forgotten how handsome and dashing he was, and was surprised to feel her heart begin to beat a little faster at the sight of him.

'Good afternoon, ladies. What a delightful day we have for a drive,' he said, bowing to them both. 'Aunt Hannah, you are looking as elegant as ever. And Miss Nash, upon my word, I must remark on the change which has come over you. You look like a breath of spring in that most charming gown.'

In spite of her determination to remain distant, Desirée's breath quickened at his compliment. She was wearing one of her new gowns today and she knew that the soft lemon shade became her very well. Certainly it made a delightful change from the drab grey gowns she had worn at school.

'Your aunt has been kind enough to provide me with clothes more suitable to my new position,' she explained. 'Though to my mind, she has been more than generous.'

'Tosh, I have given you no more than is necessary,' Lady Charlton assured her. 'I was not about to have you accompanying me all around London wearing dreary outfits in grey and brown, but I have not been at all extravagant. That outfit, for example, is in a pretty enough shade, but the quality of the fabric is inferior to what I would have purchased for myself. However, I felt that for a companion it would suffice.'

Desirée tactfully hid her amusement. Lady Charlton constantly tried to downplay her role as ben-efactor but the truth of it was, Desirée knew she would never be able to thank the woman enough for all that she had done. Her wage was exceedingly generous, and the work Desirée did was more a pleasure than anything else. She enjoyed talking to Lady Charlton and had discovered that her employer was possessed of an agile mind and a quick wit. As far as Desirée was concerned, time spent in her company was a delight rather than a duty. Now if she could just come to terms with her past, all would be well.

Unfortunately, as Desirée sat next to Lady Charlton in the elegant barouche on the way to the park, she knew it was unlikely that she would. The memory of her humiliation at Lord Perry's hands was still too fresh in her mind, and she had a feeling it would stay that way for some time.

'You look very deep in thought, Miss Nash,' Sebastian observed suddenly. 'Are you lost in the words of some ancient Greek philosopher or just musing about your next social engagement?'

Desirée laughed softly. 'Indeed, my lord, on such a lovely afternoon as this, I can assure you that my thoughts were not on academic matters of any kind.'

'I am glad to hear it,' Lady Charlton commented. 'A well-rounded mind is all very well, but to have nothing of a more frivolous nature to contemplate would make life decidedly dull. Young people must have their diversions. For that reason, I have decided that we will attend Lady Rumsden's ball on Thursday evening. She is celebrating the engagement of her eldest daughter, and there will be plenty of young people about. Sebastian, if you are not otherwise engaged, I should be pleased for your escort.'

'I am, as ever, at your service, Aunt Hannah,' Sebastian replied urbanely. 'And I should be more than pleased to accompany you both.'

Both? Desirée felt a quick stab of alarm. 'But surely you will not require my presence at such a grand occasion, Lady Charlton? You will have Lord Buckworth to keep you company, as well as many of your friends.'

'Yes, all of whom will be far too eager to talk about the same boring old things, Miss Nash. Society lives for gossip, I do not. No, I shall require your company even more on an occasion such as that. Which reminds me, we must call on Madame Félice as soon as possible. You will need a gown.'

'Madame Félice?' Desirée looked confused. 'But I thought the modiste's name was Mrs Abernathy.'

'Mrs Abernathy is all very well for day dresses and more simple gowns, Miss Nash, but a lady goes to Madame Félice when she wants something truly superb. The woman is a sensation in London. She creates the most marvellous gowns, and in the most sumptuous of fabrics. She is, however, very selective of her clientele and does not accept just anyone.'

'But I already have more than enough gowns, my lady,' Desirée objected. 'And I certainly have no need for anything elaborate. The blue silk or the pale green sarsenet will do very well, I am sure.'

But Lady Charlton would brook no argument. 'Those are pretty enough for a musicale or a soirée, Miss Nash, but they are not appropriate for a ball, and certainly not for one given by Lady Rumsden.'

Sebastian glanced at Desirée with interest. 'Do you

not wish to attend an elegant ball dressed in a gown created by one of the finest dressmakers in London, Desirée? You might find yourself being heralded as a diamond of the first water.'

For a moment, Desirée felt a mindless rush of panic. She had no wish to be noticed, let alone fêted. What if she were to bump into someone who knew of her?

'I have never sought attention, Lord Buckworth,' she said anxiously, 'and as your aunt's companion, I seek it even less.'

'Rest easy, Miss Nash, we shall not stay long,' Lady Charlton assured her. 'But Lady Rumsden is a good friend and I should enjoy the chance for a coze. And I dare say it will make a pleasant change for you. You must be tired of sitting at home talking to me all the time.'

Her assurances did little to calm Desirée's worries. The lady had no idea how much she dreaded the prospect of moving about at a society ball. The more people that were there, the greater her chances of being recognized, and ultimately exposed.

And as far as the offer of a new gown went, it was very flattering to be told that she was to visit one of London's foremost modistes, and that she was possibly to receive a gown which would put everything else she owned to shame, but what would be the cost of such an elaborate creation? Lady Charlton had already bought her an extensive wardrobe which consisted of more clothes than she could possibly wear. And she always did so with the justification that the gowns and the riding habits, the carriage dresses and the morning gowns, not to mention the fans, gloves, shoes and reticules were all a necessary part of any companion's wardrobe.

The problem in Desirée's mind was, where did necessity end—and charity begin?

The Gown, as Desirée came to think of it, was nothing short of magnificent. The renowned Madame Félice had created it herself from a length of rich, amethyst velvet, saying that the vibrant hue toned perfectly with Desirée's delicate complexion. Silk gloves of a matching hue covered her slender arms, while dainty amethyst slippers trimmed with lace encased her feet.

On the evening of Lady Rumsden's ball, Lady Charlton sent her own maid to dress Desirée's hair, and the result was nothing short of astonishing. She had taken Desirée's soft, honey-brown hair and swept it up on top of her head, then wound a ribbon of amethyst silk through the richly glowing curls. As a finishing touch, she had secured the style with a glittering amethyst comb; an unexpected gift from Lady Charlton.

To Sebastian, standing at the bottom of the stairs and watching Desirée come towards him, she looked even more like a goddess than she had upon the occasion of their first meeting. The ripe fullness of her breasts rose above the bodice of the low-cut gown, bringing back vivid memories of her standing in the patch of sunlight beside the Steep Wood pool. Her bare arms and shoulders glowed like cream against the richness of the amethyst velvet and her lips, softly parted in anticipation of the evening, seemed to offer a sweet invitation.

And for an instant, just for an instant, Sebastian regretted the impulse which had compelled him to let Desirée go. He was startled at the unexpected rush of desire he felt for her, and at the longing he felt to hold her in his arms. It was a long time since he had been moved by the beauty of a woman to such a degree.

But when she smiled at him in that sweet, breathless way of hers, Sebastian knew he could never have made her his mistress. Desirée Nash was too much a lady in far too many ways.

'You look stunning,' he said as she drew level with him. 'Truly, you will be the belle of the ball this evening.'

'Sebastian, I must ask you to stop putting such ideas in the young lady's head,' Lady Charlton said sharply. She had emerged from her sitting-room, elegantly gowned and ready to go, and now surveyed her companion's appearance with a discerning eye. 'Miss Nash is my companion and quite content to be so.'

'Of course,' Sebastian said smoothly. 'But she is an exceptionally beautiful companion all the same, and people will talk.'

'Of course they will, I would not expect them to do otherwise.' Lady Charlton's eyes softened slightly. 'You look very well, my dear. I vow, Madame Félice has a skill beyond that of any modiste I have ever encountered.'

Desirée dropped her employer a graceful curtsey.

'I have you to thank for my appearance, Lady Charlton. And for the most unexpected gift of this lovely comb,' she said, touching her hand to the back of her head.

'Well, I thought someone might as well wear it,' Lady Charlton said in an offhand manner. 'The style is far too delicate for me. I cannot think what possessed me to buy it in the first place. I never have been partial to amethysts.'

'Your momentary weakness was Miss Nash's gain, Aunt,' Sebastian said gallantly. Then, holding out his arm to both ladies, he smiled and said, 'Shall we go?'

Desirée had never been invited to such a fine house before, nor had she ever been part of such an elegant assembly. Ladies dressed in finery equal to her own drifted about the room, while dashing gentlemen resplendent in formal black attire moved among them. Thousands of candles placed in overhead chandeliers and wall sconces bathed the room in a warm, golden light, and the sweet perfume of flowers hung in the air.

To Desirée, standing in the shadow of Lady Charlton and her nephew, it was truly a magical sight. 'It is almost too breathtaking for words,' she murmured.

'As are you, Desirée,' Sebastian whispered in her ear. 'I daresay there will be many people wondering at your identity tonight.'

Desirée nibbled anxiously at her bottom lip. She had already noticed the curious glances being sent her way, and began to think she should have insisted on staying at home. But it was too late for that now. She was here as Lady Charlton's companion, and the least she could do was act the part.

'As I told you, I have no desire for such recognition,' Desirée said, trying to ignore the nervous flutterings in her stomach.

'Perhaps not, but I fear it will come regardless.'

After passing through the receiving line, Lady Charlton and her party moved slowly through the crowded room, stopping here and there to have a word with a friend, or to nod a greeting to an acquaintance.

'Before you are besieged by fawning young gentlemen intent on discovering your identity, might I beg the pleasure of a dance?'

Desirée glanced at Sebastian in alarm. 'I do not think that would be appropriate, my lord. I am not here as a guest.'

'No, you are here as the companion of a guest, and one who really has no need of your services this evening. And it would be foolish to stand idle along the wall when that is the case. See there, even now Aunt Hannah is engaged with Lord and Lady Merton, and I can assure you that once she and Lady Rumsden get together, they will be chatting for some time. So, I shall ask you once again. Will you grant me the honour of a dance?'

Desirée sighed. She wanted to dance with Sebastian very much, but did she dare? What would society think of a lady's companion dancing with a lord?

'No, I am sorry, Lord Buckworth,' Desirée said reluctantly. 'I do not think it would be correct.'

Sebastian frowned in annoyance. 'I am not at all pleased with your answer, Desirée. Nor by this insistence of yours at addressing me by my title. I thought we had agreed that when we were alone, you would call me Sebastian and I would call you Desirée.'

'That was true when our relationship was to have been of a different nature, my lord,' Desirée informed him. 'But now that our circumstances have changed, it is not fitting that I address you by your Christian name. Nor that you address me by mine.'

'Ah, Desirée,' Sebastian murmured close to her ear. 'I do not think I shall ever be able to think of you as plain Miss Nash, whatever the circumstances we happen to find ourselves in. You will forever be Aphrodite to me. And I would like to think that because of the nature of our first meeting, you would have felt at ease calling me by my name. Come say it, Desirée. Let me hear my name whispered upon your lips.'

A curious swooping sensation in the pit of Desirée's stomach halted her words and brought the blood rushing to her cheeks. His voice was so sweetly persuasive—but the smile playing about his sensuous lips so decidedly wicked, that Desirée frowned at him in mock annoyance. 'Now you are trying to discomfort me, Lord Buckworth, and I will not have it. You must call me Miss Nash and I shall call you Lord Buckworth. Any other form of address is quite unacceptable.'

'To the ears of polite society, perhaps, but I am not concerned with such things. Neither, I thought, would be a lady who was willing to shed her clothes and swim in the River Steep in the middle of the afternoon.'

Suddenly, Desirée's lips trembled with an urge to laugh. 'Lord Buckworth, I *wish* you would not keep reminding me of the folly of our first meeting.'

'I will as long as it continues to bring such a lovely pink flush to your cheeks.'

'I should have remained at school that afternoon.'

'Then you would not be standing here flirting with me.'

'I am not flirting with you, sir!'

'There, that is better,' Sebastian said with satisfaction. 'I prefer to see you with a sparkle in your eyes and defiance in your tone, than to hear you going about meek and mild and in fear of what society has to say. You are not like other women, Desirée. You never will be. You have passion in your heart and adventure in your soul. Who else would have agreed to be my mistress simply in order to change her life? You should celebrate that uniqueness as much as I do. Now come and dance with me.'

As much as she wanted to ignore his teasing remarks, Desirée knew that she could not. Just being around Sebastian set her pulse to racing. His conversation was so stimulating, and certainly, his appreciation of her was flattering in the extreme.

'My lord. Whatever the nature of our…past relationship, and however much you might feel I have qualities which other ladies do not, I would ask you to be mindful of the circumstances in which we find ourselves now. You are Lady Charlton's nephew and I am her companion. And in the eyes of society, you will be seen as paying too much attention to a servant.'

'Bother society!'

'All very well to say, my lord, but do you see the faces of the ladies around us? Look closely. Even now, they are watching us from behind the cover of their fans.'

Sebastian did not bother to look. 'I care little enough for what society thinks about me, Desirée. But I do care about *your* feelings, and for that reason alone, I shall leave you. But I shall be back, and I will ask you again for the pleasure of a dance. You shall not escape me so easily, Aphrodite.'

With that, he offered her a formal bow, a mischievous smile, and then moved off to seek other acquaintances.

In spite of herself, Desirée had to smile. Lady Charlton was right. Sebastian Moore was a terribly likeable rogue—and a devastatingly handsome one at that. His massive shoulders strained at the seams of the tailored black coat he wore and he carried himself with such commanding presence that people invariably moved aside to let him pass.

But it was truly more the character of the man which had her senses spinning. Sebastian possessed a gentle heart and a depth of sincerity seldom to be found among the dandies and fops of London society. He was exactly who he appeared to be. And Desirée knew she would have been lying if she'd said she wasn't grateful for a job that caused her frequently to be in his company.

She turned with a smile of bemusement on her

lips—only to feel it freeze solid when she saw the man standing before her.

'Well, this is a most pleasant surprise,' Lord Perry said smoothly. 'We meet again, Miss Nash.'

For Desirée, time suddenly seemed to stop—and go tumbling backwards. In that instant, she was once again trapped in the darkness with a man intent on her ruination. She felt the oppressive weight of Lord Perry's body against hers, heard the sound of her gown ripping, and remembered the loathsome touch of his hands on the softness of her skin.

Desirée felt the trembling begin deep in the pit of her stomach and prayed that she would not faint. 'Lord…Perry.'

'My daughter informed me that you were no longer at Guarding's, but I was not aware you had removed to Town.'

The peer's smile was as confident as it had always been; his manner that of a man completely in control. Desirée had to fight back the urge to run as far away from him as she could. 'No. Very few people did.' She knew that Lord Perry was waiting for an explanation, but she would see him in hell before he would have one from her. As far as she was concerned, the less this repulsive man knew about her and her life, the better. 'Now if you will excuse me—'

'I do not believe you have met my wife, Miss Nash,' Lord Perry cut in smoothly. 'Permit me to make you known to her.'

Desirée's composure was little more than a fragile shell around her. In her agitation, she had not noticed the tall, slender woman who was standing just behind Lord Perry. A woman as beautiful as any in the room, but one whose dark eyes were filled with suspicion as her husband turned to draw her forward. 'Lydia, my dear, this is Miss Nash. One of Elizabeth's teachers at the Guarding Academy. Miss Nash, my lovely wife, Lydia.'

Because she had no choice, Desirée curtseyed gracefully. 'Lady Perry.'

'Miss Nash.' The lady's greeting was as reserved as her manner. 'How can it be that a schoolmistress from Steep Abbot should come to be a guest at a London ball? Should you not be at school?'

There was a note of accusation in the woman's voice, and Desirée stiffened. 'I am no longer employed by Mrs Guarding, Lady Perry. I reside in London now.'

Lady Perry's eyes widened in surprise. 'Do you indeed? My, my, quite a change in circumstances for a woman of your position.' She glanced coldly at her husband. 'I wonder how such a thing came to pass?'

It was an agonizing and humiliating moment for Desirée. She had no way of knowing whether Lady Perry suspected the nature of her husband's conduct towards her, for while she doubted that Lord Perry would have told her, she was not at all sure that Elizabeth would not.

Thankfully, Lady Charlton chose that moment to make a most timely entrance.

'Ah, Miss Nash, there you are. I have been looking for you.' She glanced at the couple standing beside

Desirée and the expression in her eyes cooled. 'Good evening, Lord Perry, Lady Perry.'

'Lady Charlton, a pleasure to see you again.' Lord Perry bowed formally. 'You are acquainted with Miss Nash, I see.'

'I am indeed.' Lady Charlton's glance at Desirée was so quick, and her smile so warm, that none could have perceived the depth of concern behind it. 'I do apologise for leaving you on your own, my dear, but Lady Rumsden was of a mood to chat. However, she has expressed a desire to speak with you about the Oracle at Delphi.' Lady Charlton turned to smile in a rather condescending manner at the other two. 'If you will excuse us, Lord Perry, Lady Perry.'

His wife managed a cool smile, but Lord Perry was all gracious humility. 'But of course.' He bowed politely towards Desirée. 'I hope you enjoy your evening, Miss Nash.'

Desirée inclined her head, but offered no reply. She could not bring herself to utter the empty words that were usually expected at such a time. Because she was *not* pleased to see Lord Perry again, nor was she happy to have made the acquaintance of his wife.

It seemed that Lady Perry too, felt no need of social politeness. She moved away without speaking, her expression no warmer than it had been at the onset.

'Are you well acquainted with Lord Perry and his wife?' Lady Charlton enquired as they themselves moved away.

'Not at all, Lady Charlton,' Desirée said stiffly. 'I was introduced to Lord Perry at Mrs Guarding's, where his daughter, Elizabeth, is a student. I made the acquaintance of Lady Perry only this evening.'

'I see.' Lady Charlton was silent for a moment. 'And…would I be correct in assuming that you do not hold either of them in esteem?'

Desirée walked quietly at Lady Charlton's side, but her formerly white cheeks were now ablaze with colour. 'You would be very correct in your assumption indeed, Lady Charlton.'

The lady nodded in understanding. 'Yes. I thought perhaps I was.'

Sebastian too had observed the meeting between Desirée and Viscount Perry and his wife, and while he had not been able to hear any of the conversation which had taken place, he could tell from Desirée's expression that she was extremely ill at ease. Her lovely face had gone deathly pale, and then reddened with angry colour. She was clearly uncomfortable with the situation and had his aunt not appeared upon the scene when she had, Sebastian would have intervened himself.

Nevertheless, when half an hour had passed and he spied Desirée once again standing on her own, he casually walked across the room to talk with her. 'So, Desirée, how are you enjoying your first London ball?'

Initially startled, Desirée glanced up into his familiar face and slowly felt herself begin to relax. She had been horribly on edge ever since her encounter with Lord Perry and all but flinched when anyone came near. Thankfully, she suffered no such worries with Sebastian. Indeed, she was astonished at how comfortable she was beginning to feel in his presence. 'It has been an interesting experience, my lord, but I will be glad when it is over,' she admitted. 'I am anxious to get home.'

Sebastian saw the frown creasing her forehead and wondered what had put it there. Lord Perry perhaps? He wished he could have asked, almost as much as he wished he could have smoothed his fingers over her brow and erased the lines of worry and concern he saw there. The knowledge that he had no right to do either disturbed him.

'I shall ask Aunt Hannah if she is ready to leave,' Sebastian said softly, 'and then I shall return with your wrap.'

'Oh, yes, thank you, Lord Buckworth, I should be most grateful.'

Desirée watched him stride away, more affected by the concern in his voice than she wanted to admit. It would do her no good to develop feelings of affection for Sebastian. They were worlds apart in so many ways and it would be foolish of her to harbour hopes that he might some day think of her with anything more but the most passing of interest. But it was so easy to like him. He was truly a good and admirable man. There was no arrogance in his manner and no mockery in his speech. When he smiled he did so honestly, and when he frowned he left no one in any doubt as to his displeasure. Desirée hoped that his displeasure would never have cause to be directed towards her.

'Miss Nash?'

She turned to see a young footman standing at her side. 'Yes?'

'Lady Perry asks if she might have a word with you on the terrace.'

Lady Perry? A cold knot formed in the pit of Desirée's stomach. There was only one reason why the woman would have requested a meeting. Elizabeth must have told her what had happened in the classroom that night—and Desirée could just imagine what a horrid picture she would have painted.

For a moment, Desirée considered refusing. Why should she subject herself to the unfounded accusations of an angry and suspicious woman? But then, knowing that Lady Perry would only continue to harbour such beliefs if she did not meet with her and try to set the record straight, Desirée relented. Did she not owe it to herself to try to make the woman understand? For surely, as a woman, Lady Perry would understand what it was to be put upon by a man.

Not holding out much hope that she could, Desirée nevertheless followed the footman into the darkness of the warm summer evening. He led her to the far end of the terrace and then bowed politely before turning and walking away.

Desirée glanced around. At the moment, she seemed to be the only one here. 'Lady Perry? It is I, Miss Nash. You wished to see me.'

'Lady Perry is not coming, Miss Nash,' came a familiar voice. 'It was I who requested this meeting.'

Desirée whirled to see Lord Perry standing behind her and once again felt anger rise in her breast. 'How dare you trick me like this,' she said in a low, tremulous voice. 'What do you want?'

'You do not seem pleased to see me, Desirée.'

'My name is Miss Nash. And I am not pleased to see you. How could you expect me to be after what happened at the Academy?'

'Ah, yes. A most regrettable incident our being discovered like that,' he said in a voice which evidenced no signs of regret at all. 'But how fortunate to have discovered you here in London.'

'The discovery bears no pleasure for me, Lord Perry. Now if you will excuse me, I must return to the ballroom. Lady Charlton will be looking for me.'

'Lady Charlton can wait.' Lord Perry's fingers closed around her wrist. 'We have much to talk about, Desirée.'

'I told you, my name is Miss Nash. And we have nothing to talk about.' She glared down at his hand. 'Unhand me, sir.'

'All in good time, my dear. All in good time. Right now we have a few things to settle.'

Desirée tried to pull free, but Lord Perry only tightened his grip.

'You're hurting me!'

'And I shall continue to hurt you until you stop fighting and listen to what I have to say.' His eyes turned hard and unyielding. 'You have a very slender wrist, my dear. It would be a pity to snap it.'

Desirée paled, recognising the very real threat behind his words. She reluctantly stopped struggling, but remained purposely cold and distant. The man might have the physical advantage of her, but she refused to give him the emotional one as well. 'Very well, I shall listen to what you have to say. But not until you release me.'

'I would advise you not to run.'

'I give you my word that I shall not.'

The silence grew tight with tension. Lord Perry gazed down into her face, and then reluctantly released her. Desirée drew back her hand and prayed it would not bear evidence of bruises in the morning. 'Why did you trick me into coming out here?'

'Because I wanted to talk to you. And because I knew that if I made you think my wife had asked to see you, you would not refuse.'

'You sound very sure of yourself.'

Lord Perry began to smile. 'On the contrary, it was *you* I was sure of. I knew that you would agree to see her, if only to try to convince her of your innocence. Which, I might add, would be a waste of time. She already suspects that you are, or were, my mistress. But that is of no concern to me. What is, is how you came to be in London, and where you are residing now.'

'And *that* is none of your business.'

'On the contrary, my dear, it is because I choose to make it so.'

'Lord Perry, I agreed to listen to what you had to say but I refuse to engage in conversation with you,' Desirée said coldly. 'I despise the sight of you and if you asked me here for a specific purpose, then state it and be done. I am anxious to return to the ballroom.'

Lord Perry studied her in silence for a moment, and

then slowly began to smile. 'Do you know, I never realised how truly beautiful you are, Desirée—'

'Miss Nash.'

'Such glorious eyes, such tempting flesh.' His eyes dropped lower, lingering darkly on the swell of her breasts. 'You make my blood boil, Desirée. You always have.'

Desirée slowly began to back away. 'I will not stay here and be spoken to in such a manner.'

'It is difficult to keep a rational head when you are around me,' he continued as though she hadn't spoken. 'When I remember how warm and soft you felt in my arms—'

'Leave me *alone.*'

'I want you, Desirée,' Lord Perry whispered. 'I want you in my bed.'

Desirée turned her face away in revulsion. 'No!'

'Take care before you answer, my dear. As I told you before, I can make life very pleasant for you. I have the wherewithal to set you up very nicely—'

'I will not listen!'

'Clothes, jewels, carriages, you have only to say the word and they will all be placed at your disposal.'

Desirée wanted to clap her hands over her ears to shut out the words. 'There is nothing you can say that would tempt me to consider such an offer. You are a vile and hateful man and—' Abruptly, Desirée broke off. She heard the sound of voices drifting towards them. Thank heavens, someone was coming!

Lord Perry must have heard them too, for he glanced towards the door and his face darkened in anger. 'This is not over, Desirée. I will have you. It is only a matter of time.'

He looked over his shoulder to see who was coming—and Desirée saw her chance. She picked up her skirts and flew past him, running down the flagstone terrace until she reached the French doors. Only then did she stop to risk a look back over her shoulder.

But Lord Perry was gone. The terrace was deserted.

She turned back around and walked straight into Sebastian's chest. 'Lord Buckworth!'

'You seem out of breath, Miss Nash,' Sebastian observed quietly. 'Were you running?'

'Yes. That is, I did not wish…to keep you or…Lady Charlton waiting,' she gasped.

Sebastian glanced towards the darkened terrace, and then back at her. 'Who were you out there with, Desirée?'

'No one, my lord. I simply went out when I grew…overly warm. Unfortunately, I lingered longer than I should have, and when I realised that I was probably keeping you waiting, I ran back.'

Sebastian watched her in silence for a moment, and then said, 'My aunt is waiting for you at the door. Go to her.'

Desirée hesitated. 'Are you not coming?'

He glanced towards the terrace again. 'I shall be there directly.'

Desirée felt her stomach clench tight. There was nothing she could do to stop him from going out on to the terrace. If she tried, she would only succeed in arousing his suspicions further. But what if he were to encounter Lord Perry? If Sebastian had witnessed her meeting with Perry earlier in the evening, and now discovered him out on the terrace—after she had told him that she had been alone—what would he think?

'Very well, I shall wait with Lady Charlton,' Desirée said, knowing she could do nothing else. She pressed her gloved hand to the pulse beating at her throat and walked as calmly as she could back into the ballroom.

Sebastian waited but a moment before turning and walking out on to the terrace. But what he saw there did nothing to arouse his suspicions. A young couple were seated on a stone bench engaged in polite conversation, Lord Rumsden was enjoying a cheroot at the far end of the stone walk where his wife was unlikely to find him, and a turbaned matron was fanning herself down by the palms. There was no one else in sight.

Frowning, Sebastian walked back into the ballroom. He had fully expected to find Lord Perry on the terrace. Because one thing had been very clear just now. Desirée *had* been in a hurry to leave the terrace, but not because she was anxious to join himself or Lady Charlton. She had been running *away* from someone. The look in her eyes hadn't been one of embarrassment.

It had been one of fear.

Chapter Seven

To Desirée's relief, Sebastian did not comment upon her flight from the terrace during their ride home. Nor did he allude to it as he bid her goodnight at Lady Charlton's door. Nevertheless, the memory of it stayed with her through the long hours of the night and caused her an uneasy sleep from which she awoke feeling troubled and little refreshed.

'Well, Miss Nash, did you enjoy yourself at the ball?' Lady Charlton enquired at breakfast the following morning. 'I daresay it made quite a change from the social life offered at Mrs Guarding's excellent Academy.'

'I cannot even speak of it in the same breath,' Desirée said, forcing a smile to her lips for the benefit of her employer. 'The opportunity for a schoolmistress to mingle with elegant society was usually reserved to the Christmas ball at the Angel or the annual summer picnic on the grounds of Lord Perceval's estate near Abbot Quincey.'

Lady Charlton, who had been perusing her copy of the *Morning Post*, suddenly sat back in her chair.

'Abbot Quincey. Is that not in the area of Steepwood Abbey?'

'It is.'

'And were there not some rather bizarre goings on up there last year?'

'My lady?'

'It seems to me I recall hearing rumours about the Marquis of Sywell's young wife running off and leaving him after less than a year of marriage.'

'Oh, that. Yes, you did.'

'There was a considerable age difference between them, was there not?'

'Some forty years.'

'And…was there not also some speculation that the Marquis himself might have murdered her? Or are you at all acquainted with the story?'

Desirée bit back a smile. For a woman who professed to have little interest in gossip, Lady Charlton seemed particularly well informed about an event which had taken place in a small village at quite some distance from London. Not that she would have appreciated anyone pointing that out to her, of course.

'It would have been impossible to live in Steep Abbot and not be familiar with the story,' was all Desirée said. 'Louise Hanslope was actually the ward of the Marquis's bailiff, Mr John Hanslope. Many believed she was his daughter, but as nothing was ever proven, I cannot comment upon the validity of the rumour. Louise left home at the age of fourteen, when Mrs Hanslope died, and then returned seven years later to find her guardian on his deathbed. The Marquis, having also gone to pay a final visit to Mr

Hanslope, met her there. By all acounts, he was so smitten by her appearance that he proposed to her on the spot.'

'Good Lord! And she accepted him?'

'Indeed. They were married at her guardian's bed-side.'

'What, as the poor man lay there dying?'

'So I have been told. Needless to say, the haste of the marriage took many people by surprise.'

'Yes, I should rather think it would,' Lady Charlton remarked with a frown. 'But why would such an el-igible young woman agree to marry such a reprehen-sible man? And one so very much older than herself?'

'I have no idea, my lady,' Desirée admitted. 'Some said Louise was so distraught at finding her guardian at death's door, that she hardly knew *what* she was doing when she accepted the Marquis's offer. Others believed she married him *because* he was old, and because she knew she would soon be a very wealthy young widow.'

Lady Charlton shook her head. 'Goodness, what fodder *that* must have provided for the prattle-boxes.'

'To be sure.' Desirée smiled. 'Of course, gossip has always been rife about the goings on up at the Abbey. Especially as regards the Marquis himself.'

'Yes, a most unsavoury character altogether,' Lady Charlton commented as she returned her attention to the paper. 'I remember hearing tales of Sywell's dis-graceful behaviour in town when he was but a young man. He and his rapscallion friends were forever los-ing money at the tables or on horses, and Sywell him-self was reputed to have a vile temper. I am not surprised his wife ran off and left him. Serve him right, the old reprobate.' She signalled to the footman for more coffee. 'Now, on a more positive note, I thought we might visit Hatchard's this afternoon, Miss Nash, and after that, pay a call on the modiste. Lady Rumsden advised me that Mrs Abernathy has received a shipment of new shawls and I am of a mind to have one. I would like you to accompany me.'

'Yes, of course,' Desirée said, though her thoughts were elsewhere.

'As for this evening, I have accepted an invitation to a soirée at Lady Appleby's in Portman Square. Letitia is a most amiable woman, something of an Original like myself, and her receptions are always well attended. There will be dancing and conversation and it should make for a pleasant evening.' Lady Charlton turned the page of her newspaper and sent Desirée a probing glance. 'Do you play whist, Miss Nash?'

Desirée slowly put down her cup. 'Yes, I do. My parents and I passed many a winter evening so engaged. I found it to be a most enjoyable pastime.'

'And were you skilled at the game?'

'I seem to recall that I acquitted myself tolerably well.'

'Good, then you shall be my partner,' Lady Charlton announced with satisfaction. 'Lady Appleby always sets up tables for whist and I cannot abide lacklustre play. I once had the misfortune to be paired with a gentleman who kept forgetting which suit was trump. It made for an abysmal evening. We were trounced every hand.'

'I think I can safely say that I remember which cards to play,' Desirée assured her with a smile. Then, picking up her cup again, added in as casual a voice as she could effect, 'Will your nephew be escorting us as usual?'

'Sebastian? I think not. I seem to recall him saying that he was engaged to dine with Lord Mackenzie this evening, and I cannot imagine him crying off from that to attend a card party. Lord Mackenzie has two daughters and the eldest, Lady Alice, is quite a beauty. I suspect she has more to do with Sebastian's visit than her father.'

Desirée stirred uneasily in her chair. 'Really? I was not aware Lord Buckworth was looking for a wife.'

'I doubt he is, my dear,' Lady Charlton said ruefully. 'But it is long past time he gave thought to marrying and settling down. I lecture him on the subject every few months. You see, he is in possession of a considerable fortune and he must have an heir. Thankfully, for all his apparent recklessness, Sebastian does take his responsibilities seriously. So when I mentioned to him that Lady Alice seemed a very pleasant sort of girl, he obviously took my words to heart.'

Desirée made no reply, but she continued to mull over Lady Charlton's words well into the morning. In fact, she was still thinking about them as she followed her employer into Mrs Abernathy's shop later that afternoon. Strange that she had never given any thought to the idea of Sebastian marrying, when it was only natural that he would. He owed it to his family and to himself to secure the line. But perhaps it was *because* Sebastian had shown absolutely no signs of a man bent on duty that Desirée had not thought him so inclined. Certainly, his *laissez-faire* attitude towards life in general made it hard to imagine him settling down with Lady Alice Mackenzie to the staidness of married life.

Or was it just the thought of him settling down with *any* woman that Desirée found so hard to accept?

'Miss Nash, a moment if you will,' Lady Charlton called from the other side of the shop. 'I require your assistance.'

Grateful for the distraction, Desirée hastened to her employer's side. 'Yes, my lady?'

'I am hard pressed to make a decision between these two shawls. Which one do you prefer?'

Desirée glanced at the exquisite lengths of fabric draped over the counter and resolutely bit back a sigh. Woven of the softest wool, either would have been a pleasure to own, but the price put them well beyond the means of someone like her. 'I suppose that would depend upon what you intended to wear them with.'

'I did not ask for a discussion, Miss Nash, I asked for your opinion.'

'In that case, I would choose the white with the green border.'

Lady Charlton's eyes narrowed. 'You prefer it to the cream one with the blue?'

'I do.'

'Very well, we shall take both shawls, Mrs Abernathy,' Lady Charlton said to the waiting modiste. 'The cream and blue for myself, and the white and green for Miss Nash.'

Desirée gasped. 'But…Lady Charlton, I thought the shawl was for you!'

'It was, but I had already decided upon the cream one, so your preference of the white made everything that much easier. Now, come along, Miss Nash. The library awaits.'

Hatchard's on Piccadilly was both a bookseller and a circulating library, and on this particular afternoon it was very well attended. Ladies perused the shelves for the latest offerings by the Minerva Press or for books of an improving nature, while the gentlemen leaned towards those offering intellectual variety and stimulation. Shakespeare happened to be Lady Charlton's particular favourite, and while she headed towards that section of the shop Desirée moved to the shelves stocked with translations of Greek and Roman history. It was a long time since she had found time to indulge her natural love of reading. Her father had kept a notable library, of course, but much of his material had been old. Here, Desirée was able to find more recent treatises, along with opinions of the learned men of the day.

What she had not expected to find was Sebastian standing in the aisle next to her.

'Lord Buckworth!' she exclaimed.

'Miss Nash.' He gallantly doffed his gleaming black beaver. 'What a pleasure to find you here among the dusty tomes. Does my aunt accompany you?'

'Strictly speaking, I accompany her, but yes, she is **over there by the window.**'

'Ah yes. Perusing Shakespeare. I might have known. She is a voracious reader of the man's work. Along with Niccolò Machiavelli.' A mischievous light came into Sebastian's eyes. 'Are you familiar with Machiavelli's work?'

An answering twinkle appeared in Desirée's. 'Wise men say, and not without reason, that whoever wished to foresee the future might consult the past,' she quoted knowledgeably.

Sebastian grimaced. 'I might have known. I was informed some time ago that you were not of simple mind.'

'Ah, but if I could not claim familiarity with the work of such a statesman and writer as that, how could I profess to know my subject?' Desirée teased him. 'And what brings you here on such a fine day?'

'The opportunity to secure a rare book by Pierre François Galliard,' Sebastian told her. 'John Hatchard knew that I had been looking for it, and when he chanced to stumble upon a copy of it in Dublin, he was good enough to pick it up for me. I came by today to collect it.'

'I see.' Desirée glanced up at him, and then just as quickly away. His proximity was disturbing, as was the way he kept looking at her. 'How fortunate.'

'Yes, I thought so. So, has my aunt been keeping you busy?'

'We do seem to fill our days. So far this week, we have been to the modiste's three times and the mantua-maker twice, we have ordered new china from Mr Wedgwood's showroom, and a set of matching tables from Waring & Gillow. Oh, and yesterday we spent a few hours at the British Museum so that I might see Mr Towneley's collection of classical sculptures.'

'Dear me, all that on top of Lady Rumsden's ball and Mrs Taylor's musicale,' Sebastian observed. 'I wonder that you have energy enough to last the week. Tell me, Miss Nash, do you look forward to a quiet sojourn at home this evening or are you engaged on yet another social outing?'

Desirée sighed. 'We are expected for cards at Lady Appleby's. Lady Charlton has asked me to be her partner.'

'Has she, by Jove? Then you must be a very good player indeed, for my aunt cannot abide people who are not.'

'Fortunately, my mother taught me the rudiments of the game and she had a very good head for cards,' Desirée said with a smile. 'I expect to acquit myself reasonably well.'

'I have no doubt that you will.' Sebastian's gaze travelled over her face, lingering for a moment on the soft curve of her lips. 'As you do...so many other things.'

His voice was disturbingly low and it affected Desirée deeply. But then, everything about Sebastian had begun to affect her of late. Even now, her heart was beating like a breathless young débutante's.

The problem was, she wasn't a breathless young girl any more. She was a mature woman of five-and-twenty, and one far too sensible to be swept away by pretty words and flattering sentiments. 'You are... very kind to say so, my lord, but I assure you there are many things I do poorly. However, I understand that…you are also engaged for the evening,' Desirée said, anxious to change the subject.

'You seem to be well informed of my activities, Miss Nash. Am I to conclude that my aunt has been speaking about me behind my back again?'

A stain of scarlet appeared on Desirée's cheeks. 'She does occasionally mention your name, my lord, but always with the utmost affection and respect.'

'Now you are bamming *me*,' Sebastian said ruefully. 'Actually, I *was* to have dined with Lord Mackenzie but a wretched toothache has forced him to cry off.'

'Oh, what a shame. Your aunt will be most disappointed.'

He frowned at her comment. 'And why should she be?'

'Because I understand that Lord Mackenzie is Lady Alice's father.'

'And Lady Alice is?'

'A young woman Lady Charlton seems to think would make you an admirable wife,' Desirée said as she reached for a dictionary on Greek mythology. She was pleased with the steadiness of her voice as she delivered the message. She was *not* pleased with the way her hands suddenly began to tremble as she flipped back the cover of the book and pretended to read the first page.

'Lady Alice. I might have known,' Sebastian said in exasperation. 'Would that people minded their own business as keenly as they seem to mind mine. Well, what do you say, Miss Nash? Do you agree that I should cast myself into the matrimonial nets?'

'It is really no business of mine, my lord,' Desirée said, running her finger down the column of Greek characters whose names began with the letter A. 'Whether you choose to marry or remain single is surely your own decision to make.'

'I have always thought so, but it seems to be a topic of great interest to everyone else. Still, I suppose we all get there in time. Even you.'

'Me?' Desirée repeated in surprise.

'Yes, you. Well, surely it is your hope to eventually marry and settle down. Perhaps raise a family?'

The nature of the question alarmed her, but not as much as did the sudden and very disturbing awareness of *who* she wanted to marry and settle down with.

'I...really have not given it a lot of thought, my lord.' Desirée abruptly closed the book and placed it back on the shelf, aware that she suddenly had no interest in Abaris, Achilles or any other mythological Greek character. 'My situation in life has not made it necessary that I do.'

'But your position in life has changed now,' Sebastian reminded her. 'And by virtue of the fact that you *are* the granddaughter of a baronet, you have every right to expect that you shall marry, and marry well.'

'Lord Buckworth, I am the granddaughter of a man who chose to ignore my existence almost from the moment of my birth. That and certain other realities of my life have necessitated my following a practical, rather than a romantic course.'

'And that is a great pity, Desirée.' Sebastian raised his gloved hand and brushed it gently against her cheek. 'Because I believe that beneath that very prim and intellectual exterior beats the heart of a young woman who would very much like to indulge in romantic, rather than practical thoughts. Am I right?'

'Sebastian? Is that you?' Lady Charlton enquired behind them.

'Damn,' he swore softly, though without heat. He sighed as he dropped his hand and took a step backwards. 'It is, Aunt Hannah.'

'What excellent timing, my dear. I was just thinking about stopping at Gunter's for refreshments. Will you join us?'

'Thank you, but I'm afraid I cannot. I have an appointment at Angelo's.'

'What's this? Have you traded your fists for a foil, Sebastian?'

A smile ruffled his mouth. 'Not entirely. I still enjoy a match with the Gentleman when he has time, but I have always found the skill and finesse of fencing more satisfying. And of late, I have found Signor Angelo's rooms to be far less congested than Mr Jackson's.'

Lady Charlton sighed in disappointment. 'Well, we shall miss the pleasure of your company, my dear, but gentlemen must have their sport. Come along, Miss Nash, you and I shall go and enjoy the confections ourselves.'

Not sure whether to be relieved or disappointed that he was not to join them, Desirée offered Sebastian a tremulous smile and then quickly followed Lady Charlton out. The temptation to turn around and see if he was watching her was very strong.

She was thankful that she had learned long ago, how *not* to give in to temptation.

The diminutive Lady Appleby was not at all what Desirée had been expecting. Garbed in a fantastic gown that must surely have belonged to her grandmother, she wore her grizzled white hair in an elaborate pompadour, insisted on wearing buckled shoes, and even sported a tiny black patch on her left cheek. And she stood no higher than Desirée's shoulder.

'My dear, I am so very delighted to see you again. And Miss Nash, you are most welcome,' Lady Appleby said in a voice that was surprisingly robust for her size. 'Now, I have reserved the Yellow Saloon upstairs for cards and we already have quite a few games under way. Lady Fortescue particularly requested the honour of your first set, Hannah, so I kept one table in reserve. I hope you do not mind.'

'I do not mind so long as I am not expected to pass the entire evening in her company,' Lady Charlton replied. 'Lady Fortescue is a formidable opponent but I find her conversation boring at the best of times. And I do not care for her niece at all.'

'Miss Gregory is a milk-and-water miss, to be sure,' Lady Appleby agreed, the mound of hair upon her head suddenly tilting precariously to the right. 'But you need spend only as much time in their company as you wish. And I doubt you will find her conversation lacking this evening. There has been considerable talk of *The Wicked Marquis* of late, and with Miss Nash hailing from the area in which the main character resides, no doubt mention will be made of it again.'

'*The Wicked Marquis*?' Desirée glanced at the older woman in bewilderment. 'Forgive me, Lady Appleby, but I am not familiar with the name. Is that a play?'

'Oh, no, my dear, it is a most highly entertaining book. It came out a little while ago from the Minerva Press, and while no one knows who the author is, most agree that it is very well done. It pokes fun at some of the most illustrious gentlemen of the Ton. Certainly there can be no doubt as to the real identity of Beau Broombrain. Or that Sir Hugely Perfect was actually a young Hugo Perceval.'

'Be that as it may, there is no reason to think Miss Nash would be familiar with the work simply because she lived near Steepwood Abbey, Letty,' Lady Charlton pointed out. 'Certainly no ladies of *my* acquaintance have admitted to reading it.'

'Nor have any of mine, but it is remarkable how many are familiar with it regardless,' Lady Appleby said with a smile as she turned to lead the way upstairs.

'You said one of the characters lived near the Abbey,' Desirée said. 'Does the book come right out and say who it is?'

'Not in so many words, but there is no question it is the Marquis of Sywell. The conduct and mannerisms of the fictitious Marquis of Rapeall can leave no doubt in anyone's mind.'

Recognising the similarity between the character's name and the real Marquis's propensity for womanising, Desirée gasped. 'Oh my! Are all of his descriptions so…uncomplimentary?'

'For the most part,' Lady Charlton said. 'Sebastian himself was made sport of as Lord Baconwit, though I tried to assure him the author must have been speaking of someone else, and his good friend Wyndham was characterised as Viscount Windyhead. And I am sure Lord Dungarren was not at all pleased at being referred to as Lord Dunthinkin. The author has taken considerable liberties, and I daresay he shall be taken to task for it once his identity is revealed.'

'Which is likely why he is taking such pains to *keep* it concealed,' Lady Appleby said, chuckling in amusement. 'Especially since he eventually murders the Marquis with rather bloodthirsty glee. Well, here we are.'

The room they entered was quite spacious and Desirée could see why it was called the Yellow Saloon. The walls were covered in strips of pale yellow silk and the drapings and brocade upholstery throughout were of varying shades of yellow and gold. Paintings with ornately gilded frames covered nearly every inch of wall and there were knick-knacks and statuary everywhere. At least, everywhere there was not a card table and chairs set up.

In a matter of minutes, Desirée found herself seated across from Lady Charlton at one of the tables, with the famed Lady Fortescue and her niece sitting on either side of them. Lady Fortescue was a masculine-looking woman in her late forties, while her niece was a pale and meek-looking thing of perhaps two-and-twenty. Desirée soon found herself in agreement with her employer as to the brilliance of their opponents' conversation. It was monotonous at best, and Desirée almost wished for some mention of the scandalous book all London was talking about.

Unfortunately, it seemed that no discussion of *The Wicked Marquis* was to be allowed to distract play at *this* table. Lady Fortescue was clearly determined to win, and after only a few moments, Desirée found herself immersed in the game and exceedingly grateful for the skills her mother had taught her.

For all their single-minded determination, however, Lady Fortescue and her niece were not equal to the challenge. Desirée and Lady Charlton handily took the first rubber, and were well on their way to claiming the second when Lady Fortescue abruptly brought the proceedings to a halt by claiming a slight indisposition of the stomach. At that point, Lady Charlton smiled, rose and thanked them for a most enjoyable game. Desirée rose too and dutifully accompanied Lady Charlton back downstairs.

'Thank you, Miss Nash, that was excellent,' Lady Charlton said in a voice of obvious satisfaction. 'I have not thrashed Lady Fortescue that soundly in a long time. I have no doubt her slight indisposition was merely an excuse to bring the rubber to a halt. You play exceedingly well.'

Desirée inclined her head as they stepped into a high-ceilinged room where a series of couples were already engaged in the lively steps of a country dance. 'Thank you, Lady Charlton, but you are a formidable player yourself. Indeed, had you and I played against my mother and father, I am not sure who would have won, though I dare say it would have made for an excellent match.'

They soon found chairs along the wall and sat for a little while watching the dancers.

'Oh, dash it all,' Lady Charlton exclaimed suddenly. 'I have left my shawl in the card room. Would you be so good as to fetch it for me, my dear? I seem to be feeling a draught.'

'Yes, of course, Lady Charlton.' Desirée rose and quickly made her way back to the Yellow Saloon. She was not particularly surprised to see that Lady Fortescue had recovered from her indisposition and that she and her niece were back at a table with another pair of ladies. But she was very surprised when she looked up a few moments later and saw Sebastian standing in the opposite doorway.

'Miss Nash,' he said, crossing the floor as soon as he saw her. 'How disappointing. I had hoped to arrive in time to see you and my aunt engaged in a battle of wits with Lady Fortescue and her niece, but I fear I have come too late.'

'I'm afraid you have, Lord Buckworth. Lady Fortescue was compelled to bring the set to an early close,' Desirée whispered, 'but I think Lady Charlton had already decided that we had made a sufficient mark at the tables.'

'You mean you won?'

'Every game.'

'My word, Aunt Hannah must be as merry as a grig.'

Desirée laughed and was astonished at how light-hearted she suddenly felt. Just seeing Sebastian's handsome face was enough to make her senses spin. 'Yes, I believe she was. But surely the opportunity of seeing us play was not your only purpose in coming?'

'To tell the truth, it wasn't. I came to collect a debt from Lady Appleby,' Sebastian informed her with a grin. 'She owes me a small matter of some thirty pounds.'

Desirée's eyes opened wide. 'Gracious, Lord Buckworth, never say that you would actually take that sweet old lady's money?'

'For your information, Miss Nash, that sweet old lady is as cunning as they come. I have seen her relieve swaggering young greenhorns of their allowances and unwitting ladies of their pin-money. You would do well to keep your distance from her,' he cautioned.

The thought of Lady Appleby being a scheming trickster caused Desirée to burst out laughing—and several pairs of eyes to turn and glare in her direction. Sebastian himself was hard pressed to keep a straight face. 'Come, Miss Nash, I think it is time we left,' he advised, observing the expressions all around them. 'We seem to be disturbing the level of concentration in the room.'

Desirée dutifully retrieved Lady Charlton's shawl and then accompanied Lord Buckworth back downstairs.

As expected, Lady Charlton was thoroughly delighted to see her nephew. 'But what are you doing here, Sebastian? I thought you were to have dined with Lord Mackenzie this evening.'

'Lord Mackenzie is stricken with toothache, so I

came here thinking to witness your supremacy at cards,' he told her. 'But alas, I arrived too late.'

At that, Lady Charlton's expression grew decidedly smug. 'That is the best rubber of whist I have played in months. Indeed, if Miss Nash were a gentleman, I should accuse her of being a gamester.'

'Lady Charlton!' Desirée exclaimed. 'I have never resorted to cheating in my life. I simply apply my mind and remember which cards have been played.'

'And you do it very well, my dear,' her employer said, patting her hand. 'I vow it will be a long time before Hortense challenges me again. Well, I suppose we had best get something to eat before it is all gone. Sebastian, take Miss Nash and find somewhere for the three of us to sit, and preferably not in a draught. I'm going to have a word with Lady Appleby. By the by, has she paid you your thirty pounds yet?'

'Not yet, but I intend to collect it before I leave.'

'Then I shall be sure to warn her of your intentions. No doubt she will find some excuse to make herself scarce.' With a knowing smile, Lady Charlton headed off to find their hostess—and Desirée found herself once again alone in Sebastian's company.

'Your aunt is truly a remarkable lady, Lord Buckworth,' she said as she followed him to a quiet table. 'I wonder that she has remained a widow all these years.'

'I would venture to say it is only because she does not choose to seek the company of any particular gentleman.'

'But surely some gentleman has sought hers? She

is such entertaining company, and under that brusque exterior, she is possessed of a very kind heart.'

'She is indeed, Desirée. Much like the young lady she has employed to be her companion,' Sebastian said softly as he bent over her.

His words caused Desirée's breath to catch in her throat. She looked up at him, standing so close that she could see the dark flecks in his eyes, and felt a pulse begin to beat in her throat.

'Ride with me tomorrow,' Sebastian said in a husky whisper. 'My aunt tells me that you enjoy the sport and I long to see you on horseback. We could go for a gallop through the park early in the morning, before there are many about.'

'A l-lady does not gallop,' Desirée said, stumbling over the words.

'A lady might not, but Artemis would.'

Desirée started. Artemis, the great virgin goddess of fertility, wild animals and the chase. She was not at all sure how to take his comparison.

'Lord Buckworth, I cannot just *leave* Lady Charlton to go off riding with you. Whatever would she say?'

'Does my aunt not give you time off during the week?'

'Yes, but only in the afternoon.'

'Then I shall speak to her about switching your afternoon for a morning. I cannot believe that she would be unwilling to forgo a trip to the shops for a few hours. But I want to hear your answer, Desirée. Is it to be yes, or no?'

No, shouted the voice in her head. *This path will*

bring you heartache and despair. It can do nothing else.

'Yes. I should like that…very much,' Desirée said, blissfully ignoring the voice. Because there was no point in listening to it now. The heartache was already here and she had no doubt that despair would surely follow.

She had fallen in love with Sebastian Moore. And nothing she did now—including a ride in the park—was going to make any difference!

Chapter Eight

The following day dawned clear and bright. There was nary a cloud in the sky and the breeze was warm with the promise of approaching summer. In short, a perfect morning for a ride.

Unable to sleep past seven o'clock, Desirée rose and donned one of her new riding habits: an elegant ensemble in royal-blue broadcloth with black frogging on the jacket and matching black trim around the edge of the full skirt. Her hat—a dashing confection of blue and black—sat prettily on her upswept hair. Sebastian had told her that he would call for her at half past eight and Desirée knew he would not be late. He wanted to arrive at the park while it was still relatively quiet, a plan with which Desirée had been in complete accord. If they hoped to enjoy a good gallop, it would have to be well before the crowds descended and made the paths impassable.

Desirée's only concern was the length of time since she had been on horseback and the chance that she might not acquit herself well in the saddle. She needn't have worried, however. As soon as she was

comfortably settled in the saddle atop Lady
Charlton's sprightly chestnut mare, she knew that everything was going to be all right. She felt the familiar
movement of the horse beneath her and immediately
relaxed into it.

'I thought as much,' Sebastian commented with a
nod of approval. 'You have the look of a seasoned
equestrienne, Desirée.'

Desirée smiled as she gathered the reins in her
hands. 'I do not know about my being a seasoned
equestrienne, my lord, but at least I do not feel in
danger of falling off as I feared might be the case.'

'You look very comfortable and pretty indeed,'
Sebastian complimented her. 'Nor do I think you will
be reluctant to gallop once we reach our destination.'

And Desirée wasn't. As soon as they reached the
park and beheld the verdant green fields rolling out
before them, they put their horses to a canter and then
spurred them on to a gallop. Desirée felt like laughing
out loud for the sheer joy of it. She had been confined
for such a long time; forced to put up with the re-
strictions of her life so that even the most simple of
youthful pleasures had been denied. But now to be
riding a spirited horse again, with the open fields
ahead of them and the man she loved by her side, her
happiness knew no bounds.

Sebastian, of course, was a superb rider. He and
the black stallion moved as one, his gloved hands
lightly holding the reins yet controlling the big horse
with ease. The wind had blown the dark hair back
from his face, and against the warm brown of his skin

his teeth flashed a brilliant white. Truly, he made her feel as breathless as the ride!

When she sensed that her mount was finally beginning to tire, Desirée conscientiously drew her in. She had no wish to tire the mare and gently pulled back on the reins, already knowing how responsive the mare's mouth was. Sebastian, however, was hard pressed to bring the stallion to as graceful a halt. The animal was obviously reluctant to curtail his gallop and put on a great show of snorting and head-tossing as he finally came to a prancing stop.

'Your aunt's mare is positively delightful,' Desirée said, observing with amusement the stallion's performance. 'Indeed, she is almost as fleet of foot as your own big brute, and she is certainly better behaved.'

'Big brute? Have a care, Aphrodite, Trojan does not take kindly to being unfavourably compared to a mare,' Sebastian told her. 'He is merely in high spirits and feeling his oats. As for being as fleet of foot, the mare would not have stood a chance had I let Trojan have his head. In truth, I held him in check so that you might not lag too far behind.'

'Ah, then I fear I owe him—and his owner—an apology,' Desirée said, sending him what could only be deemed a flirtatious glance. 'For certainly it was not my intent to injure either with my observation.'

After the exhilaration of the gallop, the two walked their horses in silence for a while, content to enjoy the freshness of the morning and to savour the peace and quiet of the park at this early hour of the day.

'How ironic to think that in only a few hours, we should be hard pressed to find room to walk our horses, let alone gallop them,' Desirée commented with a smile.

'That is why morning has always been my favourite time of day. When the mist is still on the lake and the grass is heavy with dew, everything seems so fresh and clean. And it is the *only* time one can truly enjoy a gallop.'

'I am so glad you suggested it, my lord, thank you.'

Sebastian turned his head, and his eyes moved slowly over her face. 'You have no need to thank me with words, Desirée, for the look I saw on your face when you were galloping across that field was all I needed.' He drew the stallion to a halt. 'You are a remarkably beautiful woman, Desirée Nash. Have I ever told you that?'

'Not in…such a way,' Desirée admitted as she likewise drew the mare to a halt. 'As I recall, your comments to me at the pool last year were somewhat more…direct in nature.'

Sebastian's eyes brimmed with tenderness. 'My comments to you then were as honest as they are today. Though, I admit, they were not as tempered by my feelings. I did not know you then, but I do now. Indeed, I like to think I have come to know…a great deal about you in the short time we have been acquainted.' He suddenly sent her a look so intense that it sent a shiver up her spine. 'Desirée, I—'

'Well, well, what have we here?' a voice cut in unexpectedly. 'The rake and the schoolmistress enjoying a quiet coze in the park. How charming. I hope I am not interrupting anything.'

Desirée felt her entire body go icy cold. *Lord*

Perry! But…what was he doing here? Was it just a coincidence that he was in the park this morning?

Sebastian didn't seem to think so. He turned to regard the newcomer with eyes that glinted like slivers of black ice. 'There is nothing to interrupt, Lord Perry. Miss Nash and I were simply enjoying a morning ride and some quiet conversation. But I take exception to your terms of address and would advise you not to use them again.'

'Of course.' Lord Perry inclined his head. 'I meant no offence. It is just that the morning air seems to agree with you, Miss Nash. It has raised a most becoming colour in your cheeks. But then, I have always said that riding is best done first thing in the day.'

Desirée steeled herself to look at him. There was nothing she could take exception to in his appearance. He was seated astride a fine grey stallion and was, as always, impeccably dressed. But it was the unpleasant curl of his lip and the mocking expression in his eyes that made her shudder. 'I take it Lady Perry does not share your enjoyment of the morning air?' she asked, compelled by good manners to respond.

'Lady Perry does not rise until noon and does so then only to take herself to the shops,' Lord Perry remarked distantly. 'We keep very different hours.'

'A pity for you,' Sebastian said mockingly.

Lord Perry shrugged. 'I find other ways to amuse myself.' His smile widened as he looked at Desirée. 'A man always can.'

His mocking tone brought an uncomfortable flush to Desirée's cheeks, and she quickly looked away.

She knew what he was alluding to; as did Sebastian, judging by the way his hands suddenly tightened on his reins. 'Come, Miss Nash, it is time we were returning home. My aunt will be expecting you. Good day, Perry,' he said coldly.

Lord Perry smiled and touched the brim of his beaver. 'Always a pleasure, Miss Nash. Buckworth.'

Anxious to escape his leering eyes, Desirée pulled the mare's head around and lightly flicked the crop against her flanks. Dear God, would she never be free of the hateful man? The memory of his words burned in her heart and brought tears of anger and humiliation to her eyes. She could not bear the way he looked at her or the way he made her feel. Indeed, whatever pleasure she had taken in Sebastian's company had been effectively destroyed by his unwelcome presence and suggestive remarks.

'Desirée!' Sebastian called. 'Wait!'

Reluctantly, Desirée drew the mare to a halt. She turned her head away and quickly dashed the back of her hand across her eyes. 'I am sorry, Lord Buckworth, it was rude of me not to wait.'

'Don't be silly, you had every right to leave. The man is a thoughtless boor and I am more sorry than I can say that our ride had to come to such an end,' Sebastian said as he drew level with her. 'Had I but known he would be here—'

'You could not, my lord, so you certainly owe me no apology,' Desirée interrupted. 'But I, too, am exceedingly sorry that he was here all the same.'

'Desirée, I must ask, how do you come to know Lord Perry?' Sebastian enquired urgently. 'And please do not tell me that you first met at Lady Rumsden's ball, because I know that is not the case. You were already acquainted with the man when he came up to you at the ball, were you not?'

'Yes.' Desirée briefly closed her eyes. 'Lord Perry's daughter, Elizabeth, was one of the pupils I taught at Mrs Guarding's Academy. I was introduced to him, as I was to the parents of all the girls, at the time Elizabeth was enrolled.'

'Did you and Lord Perry have much occasion to speak to each other?'

Desirée swallowed hard. 'I saw Lord Perry… several times at the Academy, but I spoke to him…only once.'

'And you do not like him.'

It was not a question, but a statement of fact, and Desirée acknowledged it as such. 'No, I do not.'

'Was he aware of your feelings towards him?'

'I have no reason to suspect that he was not.'

'Then why did he seek you out at Lady Rumsden's ball?'

Desirée faltered. 'He…wished to make me known to his wife.'

'I see.' Sebastian's blue eyes pierced the distance between them. 'Does it not seem strange to you that a man who knew of your enmity would wish to introduce you to his wife?'

'In all honesty, I did not stop to think about it at the time,' Desirée told him distantly. 'I turned around to find him standing behind me and realised moments later that Lady Perry was with him. I suppose it would have been rude had he not introduced her, given that he and I were obviously acquainted. But now, I think you are correct, Lord Buckworth, we should be returning home,' Desirée said, abruptly gathering the reins. 'Your aunt will surely be wondering where I am.'

With that, she pressed her heel into the mare's side and set her off at a brisk trot.

Sebastian sighed and fell in behind her. He knew that Desirée was hiding something about her relationship with Lord Perry, but he also knew that badgering her would do no good. Whatever had happened between them was obviously a source of pain, and he sensed that it was something she would not talk about easily. Which meant that he would have to find out for himself what had happened.

With that grim thought in mind, he turned and headed back to Mayfair.

The next few days seemed interminable for Desirée. She accompanied Lady Charlton to a Venetian breakfast the next day and to a musicale the following evening, but her thoughts were too much on Sebastian to allow her any kind of enjoyment of either event.

He had said little to her on the ride home from the park. Had he been wondering, perhaps, at the nature of the relationship between herself and Lord Perry? She could not blame him if he had. Her disgust of the man had been all too evident, and it would only have been natural for Sebastian to question what had caused it to be so in the first place. Especially when she had not offered any logical explanation for her dislike.

'Miss Nash, you are remarkably quiet this evening,' Lady Charlton commented with a frown. 'It is not like you to be so distracted when I am speaking to you.'

Desirée flushed in embarrassment. 'Lady Charlton, forgive me. I fear I have been rather preoccupied of late.'

'Yes, but the question, my dear, is why—or by whom,' she said wryly. 'I am beginning to wonder if some handsome gentleman has not captured your heart.'

The words were so close to the truth that Desirée hardly knew where to look. Had Lady Charlton guessed her secret? She could not bear to think that she had. What would the lady think if she were to learn that her companion had fallen in love with her nephew?

'Lady Charlton, I think I shall go and fetch some punch,' Desirée said, abruptly rising to her feet. 'I find it…exceedingly warm of a sudden. Do you not agree?'

'Well, I am comfortable enough,' the lady said, 'though the temperature has risen to be sure. But I would not turn down a glass of punch regardless, my dear. Thank you for offering.'

Desirée quickly turned and headed into the next room, where a number of couples were gathering to dance. She smiled at a lady she remembered having been introduced to at Lady Rumsden's ball, and then made her way to the large silver punch-bowl. Her cheeks were still burning from Lady Charlton's untimely comment about the likelihood of a gentleman stealing her heart, and in the absence of a cool cloth to press against them, she picked up a gleaming silver cup and placed that against her cheek instead.

'Well, fortune seems to be smiling upon me yet again,' Lord Perry said from behind her. 'She has a way of putting you in my path at the most convenient of times.'

The cup slipped from Desirée's fingers. It landed on the edge of the table and clattered to the floor, drawing the attention of every eye in the room. Desirée groaned as she bent to pick it up.

'Lord Perry. I am beginning to think that you are following me.' She set the cup on the table and smiled apologetically at her audience.

Lord Perry smiled too, but with superiority rather than apology in his air. 'Nothing so evil as that, I can assure you. Your role as companion to Lady Charlton simply affords us the opportunity of attending the same social gatherings. If it *was* in my mind to pursue you, however, the outcome would be much the same. I can be very persistent when I feel it is worth my while. And you, my dear, are very much worth my while.'

'Lord Perry, what will it take to convince you that I have no wish to become involved with you?' Desirée said coldly.

His thin smile flashed. 'You cannot, my dear, because while serving as a lady's companion must be eminently preferable to being a teacher at a girls' school, it will not allow you the kind of privileges I can give you if you consent to be my mistress.'

'You are sadly mistaken if you think I long for such privileges.'

'But they could be yours nevertheless. All it would take is one word from you.'

Desirée shuddered at the thought. 'Lord Perry, let me be very clear. There is nothing you can say that would induce me to become your mistress. I am very happy with the circumstances of my life and I have no wish to change them. Lady Charlton is a kind and generous employer and I am provided with all that I require.'

'But what about pleasure, Desirée? Lady Charlton cannot give you the type of pleasure to be found in the arms of an experienced lover.'

'Neither can you, Lord Perry. And now I would thank you to leave me *alone*.'

Lord Perry smiled and let his gaze roam absently around the room. 'I wonder, Miss Nash, if your reticence to become my mistress has anything to do with a certain gentleman I found you riding with in the park the other morning. Perhaps you are hoping to receive a similar offer from him?'

Desirée's heart skipped a beat. 'You are quite mistaken, sir. My relationship with Lord Buckworth is nothing of the kind.'

'But you admit that you do *have* a relationship with him. Or perhaps, that you would like to.'

'My *acquaintance* with Lord Buckworth is no concern of yours,' Desirée said stiffly. 'Nor is any other aspect of my life.'

'Of course not. But I should tell you, my dear, that if you are hoping to receive a respectable offer from

Buckworth, or from any other gentleman for that matter, you would do well to think again.'

'Is that a threat, Lord Perry?'

He shrugged with deceptive nonchalance. 'Not at all. I am simply stating the facts as I see them.'

Desirée sighed, all too aware of where this was going. 'Lord Perry, I know that it is within your power to destroy whatever reputation I have left in London, just as you destroyed the one I had at Guarding's—'

'Oh no, my dear, I did nothing to ruin your reputation at Guarding's. That was done long before I appeared on the scene.'

Desirée frowned. 'What are you talking about?'

Lord Perry slowly began to smile. 'Desirée, you are a beautiful and desirable woman, but I would hardly have gone to the trouble of travelling all the way to Steep Abbot if I did not think it would be worth my while.'

'Now you are not making sense,' she said in annoyance. 'Surely your only reason for going to Steep Abbot was to visit your daughter.'

'That was my *excuse* for going to Steep Abbot. It was not my *reason* for doing so.'

A shadow of alarm touched her face. 'I have…no idea what you're talking about,' she whispered.

'I am talking about Lord Buckworth and the story he told as to how he found you swimming naked in a secluded woodland pool.'

'W-what?'

'And about what happened *after* he joined you in the water.'

Desirée felt the colour slowly drain from her face. 'You are *lying*!'

'Am I?' Lord Perry laughed softly. 'Then why don't you ask him for yourself?'

Desirée quickly looked away from him, aware of a roaring in her ears that drowned out every other sound. *No. Not Sebastian. Surely he would not have done this…*

'I see that my news has startled you,' Lord Perry murmured. 'Forgive me, I did not mean to destroy whatever illusions you might have of the fellow. But neither was I willing to have you think that I alone was responsible for bringing you to your current situation.'

Desirée stared up at him with a mixture of horror and disbelief. 'When did…Lord Buckworth tell you about this?'

'I believe it was towards the end of last summer. And he didn't tell me. I had it from another chap who'd heard Buckworth talking about it at his club. Apparently he related the story with considerable enjoyment.'

'But Lord Buckworth didn't know who I was,' Desirée said, grasping at straws. 'I never told him my name. So why would you or anyone else assume that I was the young woman about whom he was speaking?'

'Desirée, do you really think a man like Buckworth would find it difficult to discover the identity of a beautiful young woman who lived in a tiny place like Steep Abbot? Especially if he was of a *mind* to. After all, I *myself* knew that you liked swimming in the river and if *I* am able to discover such things, why would you think Buckworth could not?'

Desirée shuddered as she stared down at the silver punch-bowl. 'Who else…knows about this?' she asked in a hoarse voice.

'Oh, a number of the gentlemen here tonight, I should think,' Lord Perry said as he glanced around the room. 'Which is why I say that you may as well accept my offer, Desirée, because you will not receive a better one.'

Desirée's heart began to beat with alarming force. She was speechless with shock; her world turned upside down by the horrifying news she had just received. *Sebastian had betrayed her.* He had come back to London and told several of his friends about his encounter with her in the pool at Steep Wood. Worse, he had *lied* about it, making it sound—according to Lord Perry—far less innocent than it had really been.

And knowing that, how could she possibly go about in society now? How could she hold her head up when she knew what people were thinking? What dignity had he left her?

'You could of course, leave London and begin life elsewhere,' Lord Perry continued pleasantly. 'Perhaps you might meet a shopkeeper or a prosperous farmer in some small country village. They would certainly not be familiar with the details of your background and they would, I am sure, be happy to offer you marriage. But they could not give you the type of lifestyle I am offering you, Desirée. And I should think a beautiful young woman like you would prefer not to have the rough, callused hands of a tradesman or farm worker all over her.'

Desirée closed her eyes to shut out the hateful sight of him. 'Please leave me, Lord Perry.'

'Yes, perhaps I shall,' Lord Perry said smugly. 'I have given you enough to think about for one night. And I am prepared to give you a few more to mull over what I have said. Then we will meet again. You can give me your answer at that time.'

Desirée was not aware of Lord Perry moving away from her. She stared down at the floor, feeling nothing but the pain of Sebastian's betrayal stabbing at her heart. *How could he have done this to her? How could he have lied about her in such a cruel and heartless manner?*

Aware that her knees were dangerously close to giving way, Desirée turned and stumbled towards the door. She had to get out. She had to leave before she saw anyone else. Even now, she imagined that all of the men in the room were looking at her, watching her, as they recalled Sebastian's lurid descriptions of how she had looked in the woodland pool. How she had been sport for a gentleman. Well, she would be sport no longer.

She was halfway across the hall when Sebastian walked in. She saw him at precisely the same moment he saw her—and watched his smile fade as he drew closer.

'Desirée, what in God's name is wrong? Your face is deathly pale.'

Desirée stood and gazed at him with haunted eyes. Oh, how she longed to hurt him. To fling angry words at him and to wound him as deeply as he had wounded her. But what good would it do? The damage to her reputation was already done. There was nothing she could say to regain that which she had lost. She could not change what had happened that day in the pool, any more than she could change what had resulted from it.

'I am…fine, Lord Buckworth,' Desirée said finally. 'I was on my way back to Lady Charlton.' *And to beg her to let me go home.*

'But you look ill,' Sebastian repeated, his concern for her evident. 'Shall I take you home?'

'Yes. No! That is, yes, I should…like to go home,' Desirée said wretchedly. *But not with you. Never again with you.*

'Shall I fetch my aunt?' Sebastian suggested.

'Yes. T-thank you.'

'Desirée, you are not well,' he repeated urgently. 'Let me fetch a doctor.'

'No, I said I am…well. I have no need of…attention. I should simply like to go home.'

Sebastian left her then to go and find Lady Charlton. Desirée took advantage of the time to gather her scattered thoughts and to try to regain some semblance of composure. Her initial shock was rapidly giving way to anger and hurt. She would hold those emotions close to her heart, knowing that she would need them to get her through this. Anger would allow her to survive. Despair would bring her to her knees.

'I told my aunt that I am taking you home,' Sebastian said when he returned to her side, 'and that I shall come back for her directly.'

It was not what Desirée had been hoping to hear. She had no wish to be alone with Sebastian, but she was grateful that they were leaving. And perhaps it was just as well that she did not have to face Lady Charlton right now. That good lady saw too much, and Desirée had no wish to go into any kind of explanation while her pain was so fresh.

She managed to say a quick goodbye to Lady Appleby but she avoided all others. And she resolutely kept her eyes down as she accompanied Sebastian outside.

'Desirée, will you not tell me what is wrong?' he said when they were finally settled in the carriage. 'I cannot help but feel that there is more to this than just a touch of illness.'

Desirée pointedly averted her face. 'I have told you, my lord, there is nothing wrong.'

'But you were shaking like a leaf when I came upon you. Indeed, you looked for all the world as though you had seen a ghost.

I had, Desirée thought sadly. *The ghost of the man I thought I knew...*

'Will you not tell me what happened tonight?'

Desirée stirred uneasily on the bench. She would have to tell him something, otherwise he would never let her rest. But what was she to say? She needed time to be alone; time to think about what all this meant.

'I received some...very disturbing news just before you arrived,' she said woodenly.

'News?' Sebastian frowned. 'Concerning what?'

'Concerning...someone that I know. A friend.'

'And what was the nature of this news? Is your friend ill? Have they been injured in some way?'

Oh yes, they have been injured, Desirée felt like saying. Indeed, they have, but in a way that can never be healed.

'Lord Buckworth, please, I wish you would cease questioning me. I cannot reveal the nature of the injury nor the name of the person upon whom it was inflicted. Suffice it to say that it has caused me…great pain.'

Sebastian sat back against the squabs and his face was lost in the shadows. 'Yes, I can see that it has. But it pains me to see you suffer like this, Desirée.'

How ironic, Desirée thought, since *you* are the one who has caused it to be so.

'Is there nothing I can do to make you feel better?' he asked. 'No help that I can offer?'

Desirée finally raised her eyes to his. 'There is nothing you can say and nothing you can do. Please accept that as the truth and leave me to myself. I shall deal with this in my own way.'

The rest of the drive home was completed in silence.

Not surprisingly, Desirée found little solace in sleep that night. She lay in her bed and stared up at the ceiling as she relived every painful moment of her meeting with Lord Perry that evening—and, in turn, of her very first meeting with Sebastian in Steep Wood.

Oh yes, she remembered in detail what had happened. How she must have looked to him that day in the pool, and how he had treated her as a result. And she closed her eyes in humiliation as she thought of him telling his friends.

Had he really thought so little of her at the time? He must have, or he would not have spoken of their encounter, let alone have embellished it in such a way. To him, she had obviously been a young woman of questionable morals, who had been bold enough to shed her clothes and swim in a woodland pool. He must have thought of her in such a way, for he had made her a proposition because of it. One he would never have made to a proper young lady.

What a pity that she had not told him the truth of her identity sooner, Desirée reflected bitterly. She could have thrown that in his face and watched his smile disappear. For as matters turned out, that was all that had been required to change his mind. They had barely reached the outskirts of London, and all she had said was that she was a baronet's grand-daughter, and suddenly, everything had changed.

Desirée realised the truth of that now. The house Sebastian had rented for her hadn't been undergoing any kind of repairs. He had simply told her that to give himself time to find a way out of his predica-ment. Once he had discovered that she had connec-tions in town, it was obvious that his conscience would not allow him to set her up as his mistress. So he had diverted the carriage to his aunt's house, and once there, had asked Lady Charlton if she would be willing to entertain her until he managed to secure some manner of alternate employment. Unfortunately, when he had offered her a good position with some friends of his, Desirée had felt compelled to turn it down *because* of what had happened with Lord Perry and the potential damage it could have caused.

How would it have looked, for example, if word had got back to his good friends that the lady Sebastian had recommended to look after their children was a woman of loose morals? Because Desirée could not be sure that such information would *not* get back to them—and that the source would not be Lord Perry himself. Certainly the man was not above using blackmail if he felt it could achieve his ends. Desirée knew that he was well connected, and even if he was not well liked, he would nevertheless be listened to. Had Mrs Guarding not done precisely that when faced with a similar dilemma? Which meant there was only one thing Desirée could do.

She would have to leave London. She would have to leave Lady Charlton's house as soon as possible and look for a position in the north or the far west of England. It was vital that she remove herself from that good lady's home before Lady Charlton had cause to regret all of the kindness she had shown her.

And that would hurt so very much, Desirée reflected as the tears began to well in her eyes. Because Lady Charlton had been kindness itself, and to repay her in such a manner seemed shabby treatment indeed. But Desirée knew that she would rather do that than subject Lady Charlton to any kind of humiliation or disgrace as a result of the company she kept.

At half past four in the morning, Desirée finally drifted into a fitful sleep. But she had made her decision. As soon as she rose in the morning, she would begin making her preparations to leave.

In his house across town, Sebastian sat at his desk holding a half-filled glass of brandy, and wondered what the hell had happened tonight.

To say that he was confused was putting it mildly. Desirée had been in a great deal of pain. He had seen it in her eyes and heard it in her voice. But according to her, there was nothing he could do or say to help ease her suffering.

'Damn it all!' Sebastian swore softly. 'Why won't she talk to me?' Had their relationship not developed far enough that she trusted him with such confidences? He had begun to think, perhaps to hope, that she held him in some affection. But after tonight, he wasn't so sure any more. She had shut him out at a time when she most desperately needed someone to talk to.

Well, he had no doubt that she would talk to his aunt. The two had become very close in the short time Desirée had been there and he knew that she would not be able to hide her feelings from her. He would just have to wait until Desirée had shared the details of her unhappiness, and then perhaps, once he understood its nature, ask his aunt if she would be willing to share it with him.

Sebastian had to know what was bothering Desirée. Because it went without saying that if he did not find out the source of *her* unhappiness, he could not know happiness himself.

* * *

Desirée found a copy of *The Times* in the drawing-room the next morning. Lady Charlton had not yet appeared and, grateful for the time alone, Desirée opened the paper and quickly found what she was looking for. She jotted down the information on a piece of paper and tucked it into the pocket of her gown. By the time Lady Charlton finally walked into the room, she was sitting on the chintz love-seat with her embroidery in her lap.

'Ah, there you are, Miss Nash,' Lady Charlton said, her usual vivacity noticeably lacking. 'Are you feeling better this morning?'

Desirée made an effort to smile. 'Yes, thank you, Lady Charlton.'

'Good. Though I would wonder, given the dark circles under your eyes. Still, if you tell me you feel well, I shall believe it. I myself have a touch of the megrim this morning and was wondering if you would be kind enough to pick up these few things for me.'

'Of course,' Desirée said, immediately setting aside her tambour. She took the list, neatly written in Lady Charlton's hand, and glanced at it. For once, luck seemed to be with her. Lady Charlton's errands would take her quite close to the servant registry she wished to visit. She could conduct her business there and attend to Lady Charlton's errands without arousing anyone's suspicions.

A small sigh escaped Desirée's lips as she tucked it into the pocket in her gown and headed to her room. Perhaps this was the Lord's way of telling her that this was truly the way things were meant to be.

* * *

Over the next few days, Desirée endeavoured to spend as little time as possible in Sebastian's company. She took to pleading illness when it came to attending functions at which she knew he would be present, and she avoided all opportunities to be alone with him. When he did call upon his aunt of an afternoon, Desirée made sure that she was otherwise engaged. If he stumbled upon her by chance, she was polite but reserved. To anyone observing them together, it looked as though Desirée was not only uncomfortable in the gentleman's presence, but that she did not even care for him.

And the sad part was, nothing could have been further from the truth. She loved him as much now as she ever had. Indeed, the intensity of her feelings startled her. And yet, how could that be? She had tried to convince herself that the treachery she had discovered within him should have changed her feelings towards him—but she knew that it had not. She had been angry and hurt by what he had done, but his actions in themselves were not enough to stop her loving him.

And the knowledge that in a very short time she would never see him again made any time spent in his company sweet torture.

It was for that reason alone that Desirée did everything she could to avoid him. She knew that Sebastian was aware of the change in her demeanour, as was Lady Charlton. But nothing either of them could say would arrest a response. Desirée continued to be polite but distant. And every day she prayed that an answer would come to her aid.

The only person to whom she had confided her dilemma was Helen de Coverdale. The two had kept up a close correspondence throughout Desirée's stay in London, and it was to Helen that Desirée confessed the details of her unfortunate meetings with Lord Perry, and of his subsequent proposition.

And as expected, Helen's letters back to her were filled with genuine expressions of affection and concern. When she learned of Desirée's intention to leave London and seek employment elsewhere, she even offered to speak to Mrs Guarding to see if anything had changed.

Desirée had asked her not to, of course, because while she appreciated Helen's concern, she knew it would be to no avail. Mrs Guarding could not change her mind even if she wanted to. Nor did Desirée wish to go back to Steep Abbot, where she knew she would be recognised by the people she had worked with and possibly made to suffer their condemnation.

No, what she wanted to do was to go far away, to a place where no one knew who she was or anything about her background. And it was that longing which prompted Desirée to do something she had never done in her life. When the letter came from the service registry saying that there had been a reply to her advertisement and would she please provide a letter of reference that could be forwarded to the prospective employers, Desirée contacted Helen and asked her to write one. Because she knew that without it, her chances of being considered for the post were non-existent.

Helen, of course, had been more than willing to comply. She had written a glowing letter of recommendation, signing herself as the Signora Helene de Grazziano, Comtesse de Coverdale, and giving *her dear Miss Nash* a recommendation that would have stood her in good stead had she applied to the Regent himself.

Desirée had shed a few tears at the lengths to which her friend had been willing to go, but beyond that, she had little time for emotion. This phase of her life was coming to an end. The next one was about to begin. She had no time to grieve over what she had lost.

And so, enclosing Helen's letter with one of her own, she posted her letter to the registry, accepting the position as governess to Mr and Mrs Bertrand Clyde, of Banksburgh House, Yorkshire.

Chapter Nine

By the end of the week Sebastian had had enough. Desirée had avoided him, ignored him, or just plain looked through him ever since the night of the musicale. And he didn't like it one bit. There had to be some way of spending time alone with her so that he could find out what was wrong. And knowing of only one way that had any chance of succeeding, he sent a letter to his aunt and asked her to join him for dinner the following evening. He specifically asked that she come alone and said that the explanation for his request would be given at the time.

Naturally, Lady Charlton had agreed. But as she sat across from him at the table and listened to what he had to say, her eyes opened very wide at finally being told the reason behind the unexpected invitation.

'You invited me here to tell me that you wished to speak to *Desirée*? Good Lord, Sebastian, you speak to her every time you come to visit me,' Lady Charlton said in astonishment.

'Yes, but you cannot have failed to notice that our

conversations of late have been noticeably lacking in depth, Aunt. All Desirée is willing to talk to me about is the nature of the weather and the likelihood of rain.'

'Well, yes, of course, I had noticed a certain diffidence on her part, but I did not think it evidenced a problem between the two of you.'

'Well, it does,' Sebastian said darkly. 'And I have no idea why. All I know is that Desirée was given some information on the night of the musicale and she has been distant with me ever since.'

'And you don't like it.'

'No, Aunt, I do not.' Sebastian signalled for more wine. 'I do not see that I have done anything to warrant such treatment on her part.'

'Sebastian, what precisely did Desirée tell you?'

'That the news she had been given concerned a friend of hers, and that she was both surprised and pained by it.'

'But she did not give you any indication as to who this friend might be?'

'No.'

'Did it ever occur to you that the friend she was talking about was herself?'

Sebastian stared at her in bewilderment. 'Not for a moment. Why would she refer to herself as someone else?'

'Because ladies often refer to someone else as having a problem when it is they themselves who are looking for an answer.' Lady Charlton picked up her knife and cut into a tender slice of roast beef. 'I have done so myself on numerous occasions.'

Sebastian frowned. 'But what news could Desirée

possibly have received that would have caused her so much pain? And who could have delivered it?'

'That I cannot say, Sebastian, for I did not spend the entire evening in her company. In fact, I did not see Desirée again after she went to procure two glasses of punch.'

Sebastian thought for a moment. 'How long was it before I came to tell you that I was taking Desirée home?'

'It must have been going on for fifteen minutes.'

'So it is possible that she spoke to someone between the time she left you, and the time I found her.'

'Oh yes, most certainly. There were a lot of people at the house that night. She could have spoken to any number of them.'

'But think about it, Aunt Hannah,' Sebastian said slowly. 'On the occasions where you and Desirée have been out in society together, how many people have actually *spoken* to her? Everyone knows you, of course, and they know that Desirée is your companion. But of the people you have introduced Desirée to, how many would actually go up to her and engage her in conversation? Especially conversation of a disturbing nature regarding a friend of hers?'

Lady Charlton slowly nodded her head. 'Yes, Sebastian, I see what you are getting at. The only people who might have spoken to Desirée would have been people she'd met since coming to London. And the chances of any of them saying something that would have upset her to such a degree is very small.' She glanced at her nephew in dismay. 'Then who else could it have been?'

'Did you happen to notice if Lord Perry was at the musicale?'

'Oh dear. Now that you mention it, I do believe he was,' Lady Charlton admitted with concern. 'He came in late; after the tenor had sung, as I recall, and I do not think he mingled much. But I think you could be right about him being the one to have upset Desirée. I came upon her speaking to Lord Perry and his wife at Lady Rumsden's ball and it was evident that she was uncomfortable in his presence.' Lady Charlton glanced at her nephew sharply. 'Had they met before that night?'

'Yes. Desirée informed me while we were out riding that she had been introduced to Lord Perry at the Guarding Academy. Apparently, all the schoolmistresses were introduced to the parents of the students at the time of their enrolment. She told me that she had only spoken to him once, but I could tell that she held him in disfavour.'

'Well, I know that Desirée was upset by his presence at the ball. And when I asked, she told me outright that she did not like the man. So it seems very likely that he was the one to have upset her on the night of the musicale. But what might he have said that would have troubled her to such an extent?'

Sebastian's face took on a grim aspect. 'I don't know, Aunt, and unless I am given an opportunity to speak to Desirée, we may never know. That is why I would like you to invite me to have dinner with you, and to make sure that Desirée is present as well.'

'I shall invite her if that is what you wish, but that

is not to say she will accept when she learns you are to be there, Sebastian.'

'She will if she believes the reason for the dinner is to celebrate your birthday.'

'But it is not—ah, I see,' Lady Charlton said, suddenly beginning to smile. 'You wish me to *pretend* that it is my birthday because you know that she will feel obligated to stay for such an occasion.'

'That is precisely what I am hoping, Aunt. And in truth, it is not such an outlandish plan. After all, your birthday is in three weeks' time, and I think it only right that we do something special to celebrate the occasion of your—'

'Thank you, Sebastian, that will do. There is no need to inform the entire house of my age.' Lady Charlton abruptly signalled to the footman. 'Grey, you may tell Mrs Clarke that her dinner was excellent. As for you, Sebastian, you shall have your opportunity to speak with Desirée. But I warn you it may all be for naught. If she has been as reluctant to speak to you as you say, I cannot conceive that a birthday celebration will encourage her to say a great deal more!'

'It is your birthday, Lady Charlton?' Desirée's face brightened. 'Oh, but how splendid. And we are to have a special dinner to celebrate it.'

'Yes. Well, that was Sebastian's idea, actually,' Lady Charlton admitted. 'He generally plans little surprises for my birthday, and this year, he thought it might be nice to have a formal dinner at home, just the three of us.'

Desirée's face fell. 'The *three* of us?'

'Well, surely you did not think that I would exclude you, Desirée,' Lady Charlton said, trying to sound as though inviting a companion to partake of a family dinner was the most natural thing in the world. 'I could not conceive of celebrating my birthday without you.'

'But my lady—'

'In fact, I would be most unhappy if you did not agree to join us.'

Desirée stirred uneasily in her chair. What was she to do? She dreaded the thought of spending an entire evening in Sebastian's company, but the thought of disappointing Lady Charlton was almost as bad. It was her birthday, after all, and Desirée was honoured to have been invited. Surely she could put up with Sebastian's presence for one night?

After all, how many more would there be before she left for Yorkshire for good?

Sebastian pulled the set of high-stepping matched blacks to a halt in front of his aunt's house on the evening of her supposed birthday, and tossed the reins to the groom with the instructions to 'keep 'em warm'. Then, jumping down from the high seat, he climbed the four steps leading to the front door and rapped his cane smartly upon it.

He had dressed formally for the occasion, wearing a superbly cut black jacket over white satin knee-breeches, white stockings, and black shoes. His jewellery was simple yet elegant, his cravat well but not fussily tied. And as the door swung open to admit him, Sebastian was aware of a state of nerves unlike any he had ever suffered before, because he had no idea whether his plan to encourage Desirée to talk to him would work or not.

She was already seated in the drawing-room when he arrived, and Sebastian felt his heart turn over at the sight of her. For indeed, she was all that was beautiful. Her gown of pure white India muslin was decorated with delicate gold beadwork around the square neck and hem, and was slightly raised in the front to display a pair of delicate gold and white slippers. The sleeves were short puffs of fabric that left her lovely arms bare, and her hair had been braided and wound in a regal coronet atop her head. But he could sense her dismay as she rose and said, 'My lord, you are early. Lady Charlton is not yet down.'

'In all truth, I cannot say that I am sorry, Desirée,' Sebastian said as he crossed the room to stand in front of her. 'For I cannot think of anyone with whom I would rather wait.'

Desirée blushed deeply. 'It was…good of you to plan this for your aunt. I think she is looking forward to the occasion.'

'I am glad to hear it.' Sebastian moved towards the love-seat and indicated that Desirée should join him. When she sat down in the chair next to the fireplace, he stifled a sigh and sat on the love-seat himself. 'Truth is, my aunt enjoys occasions which allow her to drink champagne and her birthday is one of them.' He smiled at her warmly. 'Do you like champagne, Desirée?'

'To tell the truth, my lord, I have never had it. My

parents did not drink, and there has not been much to celebrate in the last six years.'

The words were not spoken in an attempt to secure sympathy, but rather to set forward a statement of truth, and Sebastian recognised them as such. He saw her glance around the room, and then watched her rise in agitation.

'Perhaps I should go and see what is keeping Lady Charlton—' she said hesitantly.

'Desirée, wait.' Sebastian was on his feet and at her side before she was halfway to the door. 'Please, I wish you would stay. There is much I wish to say to you.'

'There is nothing that needs to be said.'

'But there is. You have scarce talked to me since the night of the musicale. And although you told me at the time that…you had received news of a disturbing nature about a friend of yours, I have since come to believe that the news was not about someone else, but about you. And even more than that, that *I* might have something to do with it.'

Desirée quickly dropped her eyes. 'Why would you think that?'

'Because since the night of the musicale, you have taken pains to avoid me,' Sebastian said bluntly. 'You refuse to ride with me, and our conversation, when you are forced to engage in it, is faultlessly polite and absolutely colourless.'

Indignation brought a flush to her cheeks. 'Colourless?'

'Yes. Something that you are not, Desirée. Something you have never been.'

'Something I have never been,' Desirée repeated slowly. 'An opinion formed, no doubt, upon the occasion of our first meeting when you saw me swimming in the pool at Steep Wood.'

Sebastian's brows drifted upward in surprise. 'What has that to do with this? I thought you resented my bringing that up.'

'I always have, but now I think that perhaps we should discuss it.' Desirée walked towards the fireplace and stood with her head held high and her hands clasped together in front of her. 'Lord Buckworth, what did you think of me that first day you saw me in the woods?'

'What do you mean, what did I *think* of you?'

'I thought the question simple enough. Did you believe me to be a household servant or a dairy-maid? Perhaps the wayward daughter of a gentleman or the bored sister of a bootmaker?' Desirée tilted her head to one side. 'What did you think was the manner of my upbringing?'

Sebastian frowned. 'I admit, I thought little enough about it at the time. I remember thinking that you were a beautiful young woman whom I wanted to know better.'

'You mean who you wanted to bed.'

Her bluntness startled him. 'It is not like you to be vulgar, Desirée.'

'And it is not like you to be deceitful, Lord Buckworth. You may have thought I was a beautiful young lady, but did you not also think that I had the morals of a tavern wench?'

'Of course not!'

'Then why did you feel no compunction about asking me to be your mistress? For surely such a question suggests a truer perception of my character?'

Sebastian's dark eyebrows drew together in a frown. 'All right, I admit that at the time I did not know you were the granddaughter of a baronet—'

'The fact is that you knew *nothing* about me, Lord Buckworth, other than that I was a young woman who chose to swim in a public place. And based upon that, you drew your own conclusions as to the moral strength of my character.'

'I drew no conclusions about anything.'

'Did you not? Then why did you tell all and sundry upon your return to London that you had had the good fortune to dally with a comely young wench whom you found swimming naked in the River Steep?'

The question was so totally unexpected that for a moment Sebastian found himself at a complete loss for words. *Why had he told all and sundry?* What on earth was the girl talking about? He had told no one what had happened that day in the pool at Steep Wood. And he certainly had not intimated that he had *dallied* with her.

'Desirée, I have no idea what you're talking about.'

'Are you denying that you spoke to anyone of our encounter in the river?' she challenged.

'Yes, that's exactly what I'm—' And then, belatedly, Sebastian remembered. Damn, he *had* told one person. Lord Hutchings, whom he'd always considered a good friend and someone with whom he could entrust details of a personal nature.

But now, judging by what Desirée was telling him, it seemed that his trust had been misplaced.

'Yes, Desirée, I did tell someone. But it was a very brief recounting of the events and there was never any mention of—'

'Pray spare me the details, Lord Buckworth,' Desirée interrupted in a cold, quiet voice. 'You have told me all I needed to hear. Now perhaps you will understand why I have been avoiding you. For obvious reasons, the subject is one I prefer not to discuss. And now, if you do not mind, I shall make my apologies to Lady Charlton and go to my—'

'Sebastian, I thought I heard your voice,' Lady Charlton said as she walked into the room. 'Forgive me for not being here to greet you, my dear, but you came a touch earlier than I expected.' She brushed his cheeks with her lips and gave him a knowing glance. 'I hope Miss Nash has been keeping you suitably entertained.'

'Oh she has, Aunt,' Sebastian said darkly. 'Very entertained indeed.'

'Good. And Miss Nash, you look absolutely charming this evening,' Lady Charlton said. 'I vow Mrs Abernathy does an excellent job. While she may not have Madame Félice's flair, she certainly has an eye for what works best for you.'

It seemed to Sebastian that his aunt was trying to move past the tension she could sense in the room and he silently blessed her for trying. At the moment, Desirée looked as if she was ready to bolt. It was only the arrival of Grant, to announce that dinner was served, which prevented her from doing so.

'Splendid,' Lady Charlton said in relief. 'Shall we all go in?'

From almost every standpoint, the dinner was a success. The table setting was exquisite, the five course meal—complete with wines and iced champagne—perfectly cooked and beautifully presented, and the appearance of the three people sitting down to enjoy it elegant and refined.

The only thing wrong was the noticeable lack of conversation between two of the three guests.

Desirée was thoroughly discomforted by her earlier conversation with Sebastian and had all but retreated into silence. She refused to meet his eyes and spoke to him only when called upon by good manners to do so. She had so desperately wanted to believe him innocent of Lord Perry's charges. Although it was difficult to imagine how, she had clung to the slim hope that someone else had taken news of her escapades in the River Steep back to London. Perhaps even Lord Perry himself, for she certainly believed him capable of lying to get what he wanted.

But she realised now that it had been a foolish hope at best. Because when Sebastian had been faced with the accusation, he had been unable to deny it. He admitted that he had spoken to someone of their meeting, and it was then that Desirée had truly felt the humiliation. She had attempted to conceal it, of course, acting in as natural a manner as it was possible for her to do, for she had no wish to cast a damper on Lady Charlton's birthday celebration. But she could not help but feel that the tension which existed between herself and Sebastian did precisely that.

The only good piece of news she received was that Sebastian was going away. But when she found out where, she was hard pressed not to show her dismay over that as well.

'I'm sorry I won't be able to escort you to Lady Chambray's ball, Aunt Hannah,' Sebastian said in answer to her request, 'but I shall be in Hertfordshire. Lord Mackenzie has organised a shooting party. I leave tomorrow and shall be gone the better part of a week.'

'A week? Goodness, Sebastian, however will Miss Nash and I manage without you?'

'Quite well, I should imagine,' Sebastian drawled. 'Especially Miss Nash.'

'Nonsense, we shall both miss you, dear boy,' Lady Charlton said. 'But I would venture to say it will be a very pleasant time for you, as I suspect Lady Alice and a number of other young ladies will be present.'

Sebastian touched the napkin to his lips. 'I have no idea whether Lord Mackenzie is inviting ladies or not, Aunt. Given that this is to be a shooting party, I would doubt it.'

'But you cannot shoot all day *and* all night, Sebastian,' Lady Charlton reminded him. 'And I am sure that some of the single gentlemen will be happy for the pleasure of female companionship.'

'I cannot speak for the desires of the other gentlemen, Aunt, but I know that *I* am looking forward to the opportunity of male companionship and conversation. In general I find it far less confusing to that of women.'

His comment seemed to bring the subject to a close, and in a somewhat subdued manner the dinner came to an end. He did not stay to linger over port, but accompanied the ladies to the drawing-room, and then took his leave of them. Before he did, however, he briefly drew Desirée aside. 'Desirée, I need to talk to you.'

'There is nothing to say.'

'On the contrary, there is a great deal to say,' he whispered urgently. 'I have no idea where you came by the ridiculous notion that I told half of London I found you swimming in the river, for it is certainly not true. You never even told me your name—'

'Lord Buckworth, please,' Desirée said in an anguished voice. 'I have said that it is of no consequence, and it is not. The damage is done. There is nothing you can say to change that now.'

Sebastian clamped his lips together in frustration. Damn it, why would she not listen to him? They needed to talk about this. He needed to find out exactly what had happened so that he could have some idea as to how to go about repairing the damage. Unfortunately, he also knew that now was not the time. He could tell from the look on Desirée's face that she had shut him out, and he knew that his aunt was watching them from the corner of the room. But he would have his answers.

'Very well. We will speak of this upon my return, Miss Nash,' Sebastian said firmly. 'It is far too important a matter to leave unresolved. For now, I bid you good evening.'

The heaviness that had been weighing on Desirée's heart all evening seemed to spread to the rest of her body. It was the last time she would ever see him, and no matter what had happened between them, she still loved him. Which was why she wanted to hold on to this last sight of him, to press it like a flower between the pages of a book where she might look at it for all the rest of her days.

'I hope that…all goes well for you in Hertfordshire, Lord Buckworth.'

'I am sure it will. I doubt anything untoward happens in the country. It seems that there is a great deal more to worry about in the city. Good evening, Miss Nash, Aunt Hannah.'

'Good night, Sebastian, dear,' Lady Charlton called. She waited until the door closed behind him before saying, 'Thank goodness he is planning to spend the week with Lord Mackenzie. He has been noticeably withdrawn of late, and he was certainly not happy this evening. Indeed, I am beginning to think there is more on Sebastian's mind than he is telling me.' She sent a casual glance in Desirée's direction. 'Are you retiring, my dear?'

'Yes, I am rather tired this evening, Lady Charlton,' Desirée said, avoiding her eyes. 'It must have been the champagne.'

Lady Charlton sent her an amused glance. 'You had but half a glass, my dear. Still, I suppose if one is not used to imbibing, it would take little more than that to have an effect. Well, good night, Desirée. Sleep well.'

Desirée nodded and quietly left the room. As she listlessly climbed the stairs, she thought how ironic it was that Lady Charlton had finally called her Desirée, when Sebastian had made a point of addressing her as Miss Nash.

In his carriage on the way home, Sebastian thought about what Desirée had told him and shook his head in anger and disbelief. To think that something so small had come back to haunt him in such a way. When he had returned to London last summer after his brief stay at Bredington, and had told Lord Hutchings about the young woman he had encountered there, he had never thought that a year later he would be regretting that confidence.

Sebastian cast his mind back to the evening in question and tried to remember exactly what he had said to Hutchings. Certainly, it would have been nothing damaging to Desirée's reputation. After all, what had he known of her, other than that her parents were dead and that she was single? She hadn't even told him her name. She had simply been a beautiful, intelligent young woman whom he'd had the pleasure of talking to while they had both enjoyed a brief dip in the crystal clear waters of a secluded pool.

Well, perhaps that wasn't entirely true, Sebastian admitted ruefully. He had likely enjoyed it a good deal more than Desirée had. Knowing what he did of her now, he could just imagine how embarrassed she would have felt at being discovered by a man in such a state of undress. Her chemise had given her precious little protection from his eyes, and he had made no secret of his enjoyment of her body. But had he truly spoken of her in as lewd a manner as Desirée seemed to think?

No, he was convinced he had not. Even then, Sebastian had felt a certain amount of affection for her. Something about her had touched him even at that early stage in their relationship. So if the tale which had made the rounds of the gentlemen's clubs in London had been of a damning nature, it was Hutchings who must be held accountable. For whatever reason, he had seen fit to take a story—which had been told to him in confidence—and had embellished it in the hopes of making it a more interesting tale to tell. And for that, Sebastian would never forgive him. Hutchings had violated his trust, and an innocent young woman had been made to suffer the consequences.

But there was still a question which needed to be answered. A question that Sebastian couldn't help but think was key to the issue. And that was, how had Hutchings come to learn Desirée's name? Sebastian himself hadn't known it the night he'd spoken to Hutchings, so how could anything he'd said have ended up being attributed to Desirée?

Was it possible that he wasn't the *only* gentleman who was familiar with the lovely Desirée Nash from Steep Abbot?

Desirée broke the news of her impending departure to Lady Charlton two days later.

'You wish to leave?' that lady repeated in dismayed surprise. 'But why, my dear? I thought you were happy here.'

'I am, but it is partially because of you that I must go. I do not wish to take advantage of your kindness any longer.'

'My kindness? What nonsense, Desirée. You do a job for me and I pay you for your services. That is not kindness. It is simple economics.'

'You do much more than that and we both know it,' Desirée said softly. 'You gave me a home when your nephew suddenly found himself in an awkward situation. And when he realised that he had made a mistake, you offered me a position which prevented me from having to go elsewhere. You call me your companion and pay me to act the part, yet you neither treat me as a servant, nor outfit me as one. And when it comes down to it, Lady Charlton, we both know that you really do not lack for companionship. You have an abundance of friends, and were you to show even the slightest inclination towards marriage, you would have any number of eligible gentlemen dancing attendance upon you. So you see, you really have no need of a companion.'

Lady Charlton sighed. 'While the truth is that I do not *need* a companion, Desirée, it is also true that I have become very fond of you these last few weeks. And when I say that I wish you would stay, I say it in all sincerity. You are a pleasure to have around, my dear.'

'Thank you, Lady Charlton. I have enjoyed being here more than I can tell you. But it is not fair to you that I continue to do so. Besides, I am quite sure that you will soon have…another young lady in the family with whom to become friends,' she said, hesitating a little over the words. 'Lord Buckworth may very well return from Hertfordshire with news of an engagement.'

Lady Charlton glanced at her shrewdly. 'Desirée, I cannot help but feel that your sudden wish to leave has something to do with my nephew. And if that is the case, I hope you would tell me.'

'It has nothing to do with Lord Buckworth,' Desirée said, hoping that she would be forgiven for the lie. 'But I think we both know that I am here under false pretences. And in all good conscience, I cannot stay here knowing that you are paying me for doing something which, had I a choice, I would be willing to do for free. Well, that is all I wished to tell you, other than that I shall be leaving first thing in the morning.'

Lady Charlton's face fell. 'So soon?'

'I'm afraid so. I am expected at my new post by the end of the week.'

Lady Charlton seemed at a loss to know what to say. 'Well, will you at least tell me where you are going, Desirée? Is it perhaps somewhere we might still have a chance to visit?'

Not wishing to give too much away, Desirée said simply, 'The position is in Yorkshire, my lady, as governess to a family with two young daughters.'

'A governess?' Lady Charlton glanced at her in surprise. 'But I thought you were reluctant to accept such a post?'

'The circumstances surrounding the family I am going to are somewhat different from those pertaining to the friends Lord Buckworth told me about.'

'Are they a titled family?'

'No, but I understand they are quite wealthy.'

'Hmm, no doubt as a result of having made their money in trade,' Lady Charlton said disparagingly. 'Well, if there is nothing I can say to make you stay, I suppose I shall just have to say goodbye and wish you well.' She got to her feet and pressed a kiss to Desirée's cheek. 'But I shall miss you very much, my dear.'

'I shall miss you, Lady Charlton.'

'Mind you dress warmly. Winters can be very harsh in that part of the country and I would not wish to hear that you had taken ill.'

'I shall be careful, my lady.'

'And I want you to take *all* of your belongings. There is no point in leaving them here, for the servants will not be able to wear them. Nor would I wish to see you go to your new position less than suitably attired. And you shall have your full wages for the month, being that it is so close to the end anyway.'

Desirée felt a lump rise in her throat. 'It is too much, Lady Charlton. I could not possibly take full wages *and* all the clothes. Surely there is someone who can wear them.'

'There is no one,' Lady Charlton said briefly. 'Take them, Desirée. Please. Your new post may be that of a governess, but there is no reason for your new employers to think that your last ones did not provide for you. And I shall, of course, prepare a letter of recommendation for you to give them.'

The woman's kindness nearly left Desirée speechless. 'Thank you, my lady. For…everything.'

'And if you need anything else, you have only to write,' Lady Charlton said finally. 'If you find that you are unhappy, you can always come back.'

It was a comforting thing to hear, but Desirée knew that she would never be back. Because when all was said and done, it wasn't Lady Charlton she was trying to get away from.

Chapter Ten

Sebastian returned to London in a foul humour, though not for any reason he could put a name to. He had enjoyed a reasonably good week with Lord Mackenzie, partaking of the fine shooting and hunting to be had at his Hertfordshire estate, and had enjoyed the company of several amiable gentlemen with whom he was well acquainted. He had even passed a pleasant evening in the company of Lady Alice and a few of the lady friends she had invited to join her for the week.

Then why was he feeling so damned blue-devilled about life in general?

Perhaps *because* of the time he had spent in Lady Alice's company, Sebastian acknowledged as he climbed the steps to White's. And the fact that it had been a complete waste of time. In truth, none of the elegant young ladies with whom he had spent time had moved him in the least. Instead, he kept seeing a pair of sparkling green eyes that smiled up at him from a woodland pool and a sweet gentle voice that quoted Aristotle and Machiavelli…

'Sebastian,' a voice hailed him. 'What a grand surprise. I hadn't thought to see you here tonight.'

Sebastian turned to see his good friend Thomas Burton walking towards him. 'Thomas, you're a sight for sore eyes. I haven't seen you around the place in weeks.'

'As a matter of fact, I've been away in the country. Just got back to London this week and was saying hello to a few of the chaps when I saw you come in. Are you engaged for dinner?'

Sebastian hesitated. He had thought to stop only for a drink before continuing on to Mayfair, but the more he thought about it, the more he realised it was probably best that he didn't call at his aunt's tonight. He wasn't in the best mood to see Desirée, nor to play the part of the genial nephew. Perhaps it was better all round that he delay his visit until the morning.

'I am not engaged,' he said as a result. 'I am only just returned from Hertfordshire myself and thought to break my journey before heading home. But I think now that I shall stop and have dinner with you.'

'Splendid. Because I have some wonderful news to share with you.'

Sebastian gave his friend a lazy smile. 'Has this anything to do with the young lady you have been keeping company with so much of late?'

'Actually, it does,' Thomas said as they settled themselves at a table. 'The thing of it is, I have just this afternoon asked Miss Dean to marry me, and she has accepted!'

'Has she indeed? And has her father given his consent?'

'Yes, *and* his blessing. We are to be married in a month's time and you, my friend, are the first to know.'

'Then let me also be the first to congratulate you,' Sebastian said with all sincerity. 'Miss Dean is a lucky young woman.'

'On the contrary, I cannot help but feel that I am the lucky one,' the younger man said. 'I only wish that *you* might find a young lady who would make you half as happy as Miss Dean has made me.'

Sebastian's mouth curved in a smile that didn't quite reach his eyes. 'Yes. Would that we all had such good fortune.'

'Well, what of it? Is there no one who has captured your heart? I have been hearing rumours about you and the charming Lady Alice. Was that what prompted the visit to Hertfordshire?'

Sebastian shook his head. 'My visit to Hertfordshire had nothing to do with a lady, Thomas. I went for the shooting. I will admit that I briefly entertained the thought of paying court to Lady Alice, but after having spent time in her company, I realise that we should not suit.'

'Not suit? Good Lord, Sebastian, the lady is all that is amiable. She is lovely as any man could wish and she is an heiress in her own right. What more could you want?'

Love, Sebastian thought as they got up from their table after dinner and went in search of more comfortable chairs. Love and respect, both from the woman he chose to marry, and to her in return. He wanted someone who could turn his house into a home; a lady he could go to bed with every night and wake up loving even more in the morning. A woman with fire in her eyes and passion in her soul.

A woman like the one who seemed to have taken possession of his heart in a way that he was helpless to ignore and powerless to stop…

'Well, Buckworth, I see that you are returned from your sojourn in the country,' a mocking voice taunted from a table nearby. 'Did you find the air and the company to your liking?'

Sebastian had stiffened at the sound of the man's voice and did not smile as he turned to address him. 'More to my liking than I find the present company. But then, that will hardly come as any surprise to you.'

Lord Perry smiled as he reached for his glass. He was sitting with a few of his friends, and while it was obvious that all of the men had been imbibing, Perry himself seemed to be relatively sober. 'You know, I have never been able to understand why the ladies find you so charming, Buckworth. Personally, I have never found *anything* in you to like.'

'You have no idea how relieved I am to hear you say so,' Sebastian drawled, 'but at the same time, it makes me wonder what prompted you to speak to me in the first place.'

'As a matter of fact, it was Jackson's idea,' Lord Perry said. 'We were just discussing the merits of certain desirable young ladies and he thought you might like to lend an opinion.'

'Sorry. I prefer to keep my opinions to myself.'

'Even about Miss Desirée Nash?'

There was an ominous silence before Sebastian said quietly, 'I cannot imagine why you would include Miss Nash in such a discussion. She is a fine young woman who is presently engaged as my aunt's companion. If you are referring to anything else—'

'In point of fact, I was referring to your initial meeting with her in Steep Abbot last summer.' Lord Perry sat back in his chair and smiled. 'I was just sharing with my friends the details of your charming interlude with her in a secluded woodland pool. And I am surprised to hear you refer to her as a fine young woman. From what Hutchings said, you were openly admiring of her charms. Why do you think I troubled myself to go to Steep Abbot as often as I did?'

The line of Sebastian's mouth tightened. 'I do not intend to comment on anything Hutchings might have said, since it seems he has concocted his own version of the story. As to any visits which *you* might have made to the area, I assume they were for the purpose of visiting your daughter, whom I know is presently at school there. But I am curious, Perry. How did *you* know that the lady I spoke to Hutchings about *was* Miss Nash?' he asked in a deceptively quiet voice. 'Because while I do not remember everything I said to him, I do know that I did not provide him with a name.'

'As I said, Buckworth, I had been visiting Mrs Guarding's Academy in Steep Abbot for some time and was aware of Miss Nash all along. My daughter also acquainted me with the fact that she liked to slip away to the river to swim, so it was not difficult to make the connection between the two. But I have *you* to thank for passing along details of your encounter with her.' Lord Perry shot him a meaningful glance. 'After all, I had no reason to think that a young woman who swam naked in the river on a summer's day might not also be fit for a tumble in the grass alongside.'

'Have a care, Sebastian,' Thomas said as Sebastian took a threatening step forward. 'I would not wish to see you come to blows with a man unworthy of your time.'

Lord Perry's eyes swivelled to the younger man. 'I would advise you to keep out of this, Burton. Unless you are acquainted with the young woman and have an opinion of your own to put forward.'

'I am not acquainted with her, but the fact that she is Lord Buckworth's acquaintance is reason enough to defend her,' Thomas said stiffly.

Perry snorted. 'What a pity not all of your friends are as loyal, Buckworth. If they were, you might not now be having to defend Miss Nash's honour all over London. Speaking of which, is it still your intention to set Desirée up as your mistress? Because if it is not, I thought perhaps I might give some consideration to establishing her as mine.'

It took all of Burton's considerable strength to prevent Sebastian from charging the man then and there. 'Come away, Sebastian!' he urged desperately. 'You'll do yourself no good getting into a fight here.'

'Stay away from her, Perry!' Sebastian warned in a low, throaty growl. 'Miss Nash will never be any man's mistress and certainly not yours. Do I make myself clear?'

Lord Perry steepled his fingers in front of his face and laughed. 'I do not wonder that you show such emotion about her. Indeed, after having the pleasure of spending some time alone in Desirée's company, I am well able to understand why any man would go to such lengths to keep her for himself.'

This time, not even Burton was able to restrain Sebastian. He was across the table and had Perry by the throat before anyone had chance to stop him.

'Now you listen to me, you arrogant bastard,' Sebastian ground out. 'If I hear so much as a whisper that you have attempted to get in touch with Miss Nash, you'll regret ever leaving London. But if I find out that you've touched her in any way, I'll kill you with my bare hands.'

Sebastian knew that he had made his point. For all his posturing, Perry had gone deathly white, and no one else at the table moved.

Satisfied, Sebastian shoved the man back in his seat and turned on his heel in disgust.

Once they were far enough away, Thomas put his hand on Sebastian's arm. 'Sebastian, think carefully on what you said tonight. I do not know this Miss Nash, but if she is a woman of loose virtue—'

'Damn your eyes, Thomas. She is as fine a lady as your own Miss Dean! It is merely a set of unfortunate circumstances which have placed her in her current predicament.'

'That being the case, unless you wish to be seen as the lady's champion, you might like to have a care

214 *A Most Improper Proposal*

for what you say,' Thomas persisted gently. 'Listening to the way you defended her would almost lead one to believe that—'

'Believe what?' Sebastian growled.

'That you…cared for the young woman.'

It was too close to the truth for Sebastian's liking. As was the fact that he couldn't say a damn thing to refute it.

Shortly after the confrontation with Lord Perry, Sebastian left White's and headed for his aunt's house. He needed to speak to Desirée. It was time for them to clear the air once and for all. A number of things had become clear to him while he was in Hertfordshire and the rest had fallen into place tonight. Not the least of which was that he was in love with Desirée Nash.

Oh yes, he loved her, Sebastian admitted. It might be the first time he had admitted it in so many words, but he knew it to be the truth. As he did the fact that he'd been feeling this way for a long time. He wasn't sure when he'd fallen in love with Desirée, but he suspected it was last summer when she'd told him to his face that she was too good to be his mistress. And everything that had happened between now and then had only caused him to love her more.

And now it was time to tell her that. He wondered for a moment how his aunt would take the news, but in all honesty, he did not think she would be unhappy. She liked Desirée, and after all, she was Sir George Owens's granddaughter.

Unfortunately, as it turned out, Sebastian was to be

denied the pleasure of telling the woman he loved how he felt about her. Upon arriving at his aunt's house, he was informed that the lady who had become such an important part of his life—the woman who meant more to him than anyone in the world—had packed her bags and left London for good!

Desirée did not settle well into her new position in Yorkshire. Banksburgh House was located on the side of a remote, windswept hill in the northern dales, and was about an hour by carriage from the nearest village. The prospect from the front window was mildly pleasing, but the house itself was not. Desirée found the dark ugly mansion extremely depressing after the airy brightness of Lady Charlton's elegant town house. As she did the personalities of the brooding Mr Clyde and his wife.

To be sure, there was precious little laughter to be heard in the halls of Banksburgh House. The only bright spot in an otherwise gloomy picture was the younger of the two girls Desirée had been engaged to look after. Miss Sarah Clyde was four years old and was as sweet as any child Desirée had ever had the pleasure to meet. Her thirteen-year-old sister, Caroline, however, was a different matter altogether. She was sorely in need of discipline as a result of having been spoiled by her mother, and was now used to getting whatever she wanted. Unfortunately, when Desirée tried to chastise her, the child inevitably ran to her mama, who then informed Desirée that it was her job to *teach* her children, *not* to discipline them.

Hence, it was not long after her arrival that Desirée knew she had made a dreadful mistake.

Still, there was nothing she could do about it now. She could hardly turn around and ask Lady Charlton to take her back. Nor *would* she go back if she'd been given the choice. Because the problem which had caused her to leave would be the same. Sebastian would still be there. He would still call at the house whenever he felt so inclined, and he would continue to smile at her in that special way that set Desirée's heart to racing.

And foolishly, she would continue to hope that one day he might see her as something other than the young woman he had discovered swimming in the Steep Wood pool. A woman he had brought to London to be his mistress, only to think better of it once he had discovered her connections.

But she knew it was unlikely that he would. He might even now be engaged to the Lady Alice Mackenzie. Lady Charlton might have already forgotten about her and be busy making wedding preparations, excited at the prospect of her beloved nephew finally settling down to married life.

It was that thought more than any that made life tolerable for Desirée at Banksburgh House. Because the thought of the alternative, of having to see Sebastian every day, and to hear him talk about the woman he loved and was soon to marry, would have been far more destructive to her happiness than anything the parsimonious Mr Clyde and his family could do.

* * *

'But did she give you no indication as to *where* she was going?' Sebastian dragged his hand through his hair again, sending it even further into disarray, as he turned to face his aunt. 'She *must* have said something!'

'Sebastian, I told you, Desirée did not tell me anything about where she was going, other than to say that it was to a wealthy family in Yorkshire where she would be employed as their governess. I did not wish to interrogate her on the subject.'

'But did she say that she would write?'

'No, my dear, she did not. I hope that she will keep in touch, of course, but I do not expect to hear from her for some time. Sebastian, you do seem unusually disturbed by Desirée's departure.' Lady Charlton's eyes narrowed thoughtfully. 'Why should her leaving London to secure other employment bother you so much?'

'Because *I* am the one who let her down,' Sebastian said heavily. 'After all, it was my idea to bring her to London in the first place, and now she has left it *because* of me.'

'What do you mean she's left because of you? Desirée told me that she was leaving because of *me*. She told me she felt she wasn't earning her way and that I was treating her more like a friend than a companion. Which I suppose I was,' Lady Charlton acknowledged ruefully. 'But I really couldn't help myself. I liked Desirée and I wanted to help her.'

And I love her, Sebastian thought desperately. And now because of him and the things he had said, she was gone.

But what was he to do? How in God's name was he to find a young woman who clearly didn't want to be found? She could have gone to any one of hundreds of small villages dotted throughout the dales. Or she could have gone to a wealthy family in one of the towns: Sheffield or Wakefield in the south; Middlesborough or Northallerton in the north. She might even have gone to the cathedral city of York. How was he to find her then?

Where did he start his search for what could turn out to be the proverbial needle in a haystack?

Chapter Eleven

Sebastian set out for Yorkshire the following day. He did not tell anyone where he was going, though he had a feeling his aunt suspected. She seemed to have a funny, knowing look in her eyes since he'd returned from Hertfordshire. But Sebastian didn't care. He wouldn't have bothered to deny his feelings for Desirée even if his aunt had asked. The fact that she hadn't simply allowed him to keep the knowledge to himself until the time was right to share it.

If, he reminded himself, the time would ever be right.

Not surprisingly, the trip north seemed endless. Sebastian had mapped out the route he intended to take, and stayed at coaching inns he knew along the way. And at every one, he asked the same questions. Even so, by the time he arrived in Kettlewell, near Skipton, Sebastian was weary of the road. He walked into the local inn and then headed for the bar, casually pulling out his purse as he did. 'I am looking to make enquiries,' he said in a voice loud enough for the innkeeper to hear.

The burly, red-faced man looked at Sebastian's heavy purse and all but licked his lips. 'Aye, my lord, and what kind of information would you be looking for?'

'I am looking for a young woman. She would have arrived about a week or so ago.' Sebastian made a show of opening up the neck of the bag and removing a coin. 'She has light brown hair and green eyes, and she is exceedingly lovely. Do you recall having seen anyone like that?'

The innkeeper's eyes turned shrewd. 'I don't *recall* seeing any young lady like that, my lord, though there's plenty of them come through here. Maybe I need a bit more reminding.'

Knowing the game, Sebastian drew another coin from the bag. 'She was going to a big house to be a governess. Apparently the family is quite wealthy.'

'Now, I could be remembering a young lady who came about a job,' the innkeeper said slowly. He tapped his finger against his cheek. 'But I'm just not too clear about which family she was going to.'

'No? Pity.' Sebastian began to close his purse. 'I was willing to pay well for the information.'

'Oh, now wait a minute, my lord, I—'

'Would you be willing to pay anyone for the information, my lord?' a young woman asked suddenly. 'Because I remember seeing a young lady who looked like the one you're referring to come through here last week.'

Sebastian turned to see a girl of about eighteen standing behind him. She was remarkably pretty and there was a gentleness about her that seemed strangely out of place in this rough and tumble place. But her face was already beginning to show signs of age and her hands were rough and reddened from hard work. 'You saw her?'

'Aye, m'lord.'

The landlord frowned darkly. 'Nobody was talking to you, Jenny, my girl. Go on back to the kitchen. There'll be plenty o' pots waiting.'

'No, just a minute,' Sebastian said, stopping her as she went to turn away. 'My money goes to anyone who can supply me with the information I need.' He reached for her hand and put the two coins into her palm. 'Now, Jenny, what did you see?'

Jenny glanced nervously at the man standing behind the counter, then at the money in her palm, and then anxiously bit her lip. 'A young lady like you described came through here late last week, m'lord. But she wasn't here long. They came to fetch her.'

'They?'

'Aye. One of t'lads from Banksburgh House. They came with the trap.'

Sebastian pulled another coin from the bag. 'And where is Banksburgh House, Jenny?'

'Now, my lord, I can supply you with that bit of information,' the innkeeper said hastily. 'You've given our Jenny more money than she's seen in her entire life. No need to be giving her more than she'll have need of.'

'Are you her father?'

The man shook his head. 'Nay, I'll not say that I am. But she's worked for me for nigh on four years now, so I tend to think of myself that way.'

Sebastian ignored him and placed the coin in Jenny's palm. 'Jenny?'

Hardly able to believe her good fortune, Jenny's eyes widened. 'It's on down t'road, m'lord, then left at Miller's Cross. It's a big place, is Banksburgh House. You can't miss it from t'road.'

'And the owner is?'

'Mr Clyde. They have two daughters, a Miss Caroline and young Sarah. It's for them that Mrs Clyde was wanting a governess.'

It was all Sebastian needed to know. He put away his purse and, drawing out one of his cards, pressed it into her hand. 'Thank you, Jenny. The information you have given me is very important and I am forever in your debt. If you ever find yourself in any kind of trouble—' Sebastian glanced pointedly at the innkeeper, 'I want you to get in touch with me at that address. Do you understand?'

Jenny took the card and her eyes grew even wider as she read the name printed upon it. 'Aye, m'lord.'

'Good. And I shall stop by whenever I am passing through the area to enquire after your health,' he added, again with a look for the burly man standing beside her. Then, satisfied that he had done all he could for her, Sebastian turned and left the coaching inn, heading for Banksburgh House.

The afternoon had turned uncommonly warm and Desirée decided to take her two young charges outside to enjoy it. The grounds around Banksburgh House were surprisingly well tended, given the relative barrenness of the surrounding area, and Desirée had walked more than once to the farthest reaches of the property. At least there she was able to escape the overbearing presence of Mrs Clyde.

Fortunately, Desirée got on reasonably well with the rest of the staff. The housekeeper, a stern-faced woman by the name of Mrs Hagerty, was accommodating if not friendly, and life on the whole was tolerable. But her spartan room was a far cry from the comfort and charm of the Green Room at Lady Charlton's. Nor were her lovely clothes of any use to her here. Mrs Clyde insisted on Desirée wearing the drabbest of garments and had provided her with two highly serviceable gowns, one in grey and the other in a dull shade of brown.

Desirée almost felt as if she was back at the Guarding Academy again.

It was wearing her unbecoming grey gown that Sebastian came upon her that afternoon. Quite by chance, he spotted Desirée and her two young charges as he was making his way up the long drive. Rather than announce himself to the lady of the house and formally ask permission to see the governess, however, he stopped the carriage at the side of the drive and made his way across the field to where she was standing.

'Good afternoon, Desirée,' Sebastian said, removing his shining black beaver as he swept her a bow. 'I don't expect you ever thought to see me again.'

Desirée, who had indeed been rendered speechless by the sight of the man walking across the field towards her, now struggled to find her voice. 'Lord…Buckworth! Yes, I confess, I am…astonished at seeing you here.'

'Miss Nash, who is this gentleman?' Miss Caroline Clyde asked imperiously.

This is the man I love, Desirée wanted to tell her. *The man who has come all the way to Yorkshire to find me, and hopefully to take me back to London.* All she said, however, was, 'This is a…friend of mine from London, Caroline. Lord Buckworth, may I present Miss Caroline Clyde and her sister, Miss Sarah Clyde. Girls, this is Lord Buckworth.'

The elder Miss Clyde seemed suitably impressed that a titled gentleman had come to call, and she bobbed a pretty curtsey. Sarah, bless her heart, merely smiled her winsome smile and held out her hand to him. 'Have you come to see our governess?' she asked sweetly.

Sebastian grinned at the colour which suddenly bloomed in Desirée's cheeks. 'As a matter of fact, I have, Sarah. Is that all right with you?'

Sarah thought about it for a moment, and then nodded, setting her blonde curls dancing. 'Yeth.'

'Good. Now, Miss Caroline,' Sebastian said to the elder girl, 'perhaps you would be so good as to take your sister back to the house. Miss Nash will be along…directly.'

'But Mama says that Miss Nash is to stay with us at all times,' Caroline told him stubbornly. 'Isn't that right, Miss Nash?'

'Well, yes it is—'

'But I am sure that your mama will not mind if you walk back alone just this once,' Sebastian interposed smoothly. 'We are in clear sight of the house and you have only to follow the path back through the gate there.'

Surprisingly, it was Sarah who took her sister by the hand and started dragging her back in the direction of the house. 'Come along, Cawoline. I think we should go.'

To Desirée's astonishment, Caroline actually went. 'Oh, very well,' she grumbled. 'It was very nice meeting you, Lord Buckworth.'

Sebastian offered her his most charming smile. 'The pleasure was all mine, Miss Clyde.'

Desirée bit her lip as she watched the two young figures retreat. 'I really shouldn't let them walk back alone, Lord Buckworth,' she said anxiously. 'Mrs Clyde is most particular—'

'They will be fine, Desirée. We are well within sight of the house.'

'Yes, I know. Which is why I should not have let them go back alone. Mrs Clyde may see them walking on their own and she has made it very clear that the girls are to be accompanied at all times.'

Sebastian took her by the shoulders and gently turned her to face him. 'Desirée, I want to talk to you. And I could hardly do that with two young girls listening to every word I said, now could I?'

Dismayed both by the touch of his hands and by the softness of his voice, Desirée reluctantly inclined her head. The thought of having to talk with him in the presence of the Misses Clyde was decidedly unwelcome, but the thought of being alone with him was not much better—especially given that she had thought never to see him again.

She watched her two young charges until they reached the safety of the house and felt marginally better once she saw them go inside. Now it was time to face her other problem.

'To say that I am…surprised to see you would be something of an understatement, my lord,' Desirée began carefully. 'You must have gone to considerable trouble to discover my whereabouts.'

'I hardly knew where to begin,' Sebastian admitted. 'But once I arrived in Yorkshire I happened upon a bit of luck. A young lady at the coaching inn in

Kettlewell remembered seeing you and was good enough to point me in the right direction.' He glanced at the scenery all around them, and then turned back to gaze deeply into her eyes. 'Are you happy here, Desirée?'

'I find the work…satisfying.' *How can I be happy when you are so far away?* 'Caroline can be somewhat trying at times, but her sister more than makes up for it.' Desirée's mouth curved in an affectionate smile. 'You saw for yourself what a delight Sarah is.'

'I did indeed. And your employers?' Sebastian enquired, his eyes turning to the nearby bulk of a house. 'Are they as delightful as their youngest daughter?'

The thought nearly made Desirée laugh. She doubted anyone who knew the Clydes would have called them delightful. 'I do not see a great deal of Mr Clyde, as he is mostly occupied on business in the north. Mrs Clyde, however, is typical of her kind. She does not put up with nonsense from her children or her staff, and I think most of the maids go in fear of her.'

'And you?'

'I know what my job is and I do it,' Desirée said, careful not to allow the slightest inflection into her voice. *Why had he come?* There had to be more to his visit than a desire for polite conversation? Surely he would not have troubled himself to travel all this way if that was all he had in mind…would he?

'My lord, I must be returning to the house—'

'Desirée, forgive me for interrupting, but there is something I must ask you,' Sebastian said abruptly. 'Something which has been on my mind ever since I left London. Indeed it was part of my reason for coming.'

Desirée found that her hands were suddenly trembling. She clasped them together in front of her and strove for a casual tone. 'And what is that, my lord?'

'Before I left, I had occasion to speak to…Lord Perry,' Sebastian said quietly. 'It was not a pleasant meeting and he told me things which I found most disturbing. Things which, quite frankly, I did not know how to take.'

At the mention of Lord Perry's name, the trembling in Desirée's hands grew worse. 'And what has your…disturbing conversation with Lord Perry to do with me?'

'It has everything to do with you.' Sebastian stopped walking and turned to face her. 'He led me to believe that the two of you had spent some time together while you were at Guarding's. He said that…after having done so, he could understand my fascination and desire for you. And he said, in front of others, that if it was not my intention to set you up as my mistress, that he would very probably do so himself.'

Desirée listened with growing dismay, until in the end, the depth of her grief went far beyond tears. Truly, it was worse than she had imagined. They had been discussing her as though she were little more than a used piece of baggage; something to be picked up by one when carelessly cast off by another.

She stared into the distance and felt a sudden chill in the afternoon air. 'And what did you tell Lord Perry in answer to his question, Lord Buckworth?'

'Damn it, Desirée, what do you think I told him?'

'I have no idea.' She turned to face him with eyes that were curiously devoid of expression. 'Because the fact that you came here today and told me what you have leads me to believe that *you* doubt my integrity as well. The fact that you would even *consider* Lord Perry's story to be the truth tells me what you really think of me.'

'The fact that he was known to you in Steep Abbot, and that you hold him in such abhorrence makes all manner of things possible, Desirée,' Sebastian said harshly. 'Because I now believe that whatever happened between you and Lord Perry was the cause of your leaving the Guarding Academy. The reason you were…asked to leave.'

Desirée closed her eyes. 'And you think that I…brought this on myself? That I invited Lord Perry's attentions?'

'That is not what I said. I am *asking* you to tell me what happened, and to explain why you left London so abruptly. God knows, I hold Perry in no higher esteem than do you. In fact, it was only through the intervention of a good friend that I did not challenge him on the spot. But I am asking you now to tell me what passed between the two of you at Guarding's. Because the manner of what Perry told me led me to believe that the two of you had had…an intimate encounter.'

His words hung heavy in the air between them and Desirée suddenly felt a coldness spread through her body, as though the blood in her veins had turned to ice. So he had not followed her all the way to Yorkshire to declare his love and to take her back with him. He had come on a fool's journey to find out whether or not a rumour told to him by a man he admitted disliking had any truth to it.

'Very well, Lord Buckworth, you shall have your answer,' Desirée said in a voice that was as bleak and as barren as the hills all around them. 'Lord Perry *was* the reason I left the Guarding Academy. He caught me in my classroom at the end of the day and he…he…'

'Tell me, Desirée,' Sebastian said quietly. 'Please.'

'He t-told me that he had been waiting to get me alone for a long time. And he asked me to be his mistress. When I refused, he lunged at me and…tore my gown.' Desirée closed her eyes against the painful memory. 'I tried to resist, but he was too strong.'

A muscle tensed in Sebastian's cheek. 'What happened then?'

'I was fortunate. The door opened and Mrs Guarding walked in. She had one of the other teachers and two of the students with her. But they all…saw me in Lord Perry's arms.'

'How did Mrs Guarding know to come and find you?'

'Apparently Helen had been waiting for me,' Desirée said slowly. 'She knew that I had planned to go back to my classroom after dinner, and when I didn't return to my bedroom, she began to worry. So she went down and got Mrs Guarding. I have no idea how Miss Perry and her friend came to be there—'

'Miss Perry?' Sebastian's dark brows lifted in surprise. 'Lord Perry's daughter?'

'Yes. Perhaps she knew what was afoot, I don't know,' Desirée said wearily. 'All I know is that she was there and that she saw what happened.'

'And you left because of that?'

'I was *asked* to leave because of it,' she said tersely. 'With two of the girls there to witness my ruination, I had no choice. Mrs Guarding had to consider the reputation of the school.'

'So that is why she did not provide you with a reference.'

'Under the circumstances, she could not.'

'And when Lord Perry saw you again at Lady Rumsden's ball in London—'

'He…asked me again to be his mistress.' Desirée took a deep breath. 'He told me that I might as well accept his offer because I could not hope to do better. And when I said that I knew he could ruin my reputation in London just as he had in Steep Abbot, he informed me that…my reputation was already lost because *you* had told all of your friends and acquaintances upon your return to London that we had been…together in the River Steep.'

'Desirée, I swear, I told only one man of our meeting in the woods,' Sebastian said desperately. 'A gentleman I thought of as a friend. But it was he who spread the tale and he who embellished it to make it sound far worse than it really was. Only think, Desirée. Why would I have gone around talking about you? I didn't even know who you were. I had seen you once and knew nothing about you, save that your parents were dead and that you were not married. From your conversation I was able to glean that you were well educated, but I knew nothing else. All I saw was a beautiful young woman who enjoyed swimming in a woodland pool.'

'And whom you suspected of having loose morals.'

'That's not what I said!'

'But you must have thought it, my lord. Why else would you have asked me to be your mistress? In truth, you are no better than Lord Perry. And it does not matter whether you told one or a hundred people,' Desirée cried. 'It was enough that you recounted the details of your escapade in the country to one man, and that you both enjoyed a good laugh at my expense.'

'Desirée, please—'

'Well, I am not laughing, my lord,' Desirée told him angrily. 'When Lord Perry asked me to be his mistress and I turned him down, he told me that he would use every means at his disposal to ensure that I *did* eventually agree. And that's why I left London. I was not willing to endanger Lady Charlton's good name. I did not want to make her look a fool in front of her friends, when it became known that the lady she had chosen to be her companion was a woman of questionable morals. I turned down the position as governess to your friends for exactly the same reason.'

'Desirée, for God's sake, why didn't you tell me any of this?'

'Because it didn't matter. What did, was that I left your aunt's house—and London—as quickly as possible. Lord Perry was waiting for an answer. I knew that I was running out of time. So the morning after Lady Appleby's soirée, I went to one of the service registries in town and applied for a position. Eventually, I was lucky enough to be offered one.'

'But without any letters of reference, how did you secure it?'

Desirée blushed. 'I wrote to my friend Helen at the Academy and asked her to provide me with one.'

'I hardly think the recommendation of a friend and fellow teacher would have accomplished what was required.'

'No, but one signed by the Signora Helene de Grazziano, Comtesse de Coverdale was.'

Sebastian nodded. 'So you lied.'

'I did what I had to do!' Desirée cried in frustration. 'I needed a position, Lord Buckworth. And while this might not be exactly what I would have wished for, it has provided me with a roof over my head and a steady wage. More importantly, it has given me a chance to start again. I came here with my reputation intact and I keep to myself as much as possible. And that is the way it will be from now on because I will not let myself be hurt again. Not by you or anyone else.'

'Desirée, I had to ask,' Sebastian said, praying that she understood. 'Perry made it sound as though—'

'Yes, I know how Lord Perry would have made it sound,' Desirée said bitterly. 'Why would he not? He has no reputation to worry about. I was a lowly teacher at a girl's school; a woman he felt perfectly within his rights to approach with lewd suggestions and improper conduct. He would not have treated a lady in such a way. Indeed, I wonder if he would have attempted such a seduction had he known that I was the granddaughter of the late Sir George Owens. I venture to say he would not.'

'Desirée, let me take you back to London,' Sebastian said earnestly. 'There is no need for you to remain here any longer. My aunt misses you terribly and so do I. Come back with me and everything shall be as it was.'

Desirée looked at him askance. 'But don't you understand what I have been saying, Lord Buckworth? Nothing will *ever* be as it was! How can I go back to London knowing what I do now? How could I…walk into a room and hold my head up, knowing that half the gentlemen in the room are seeing me as

Lord Perry does? Wondering, perhaps, if I would agree to be *their* mistress, if I would not be his—or yours?'

'You will be no man's mistress, Desirée,' Sebastian growled, 'and you will have nothing to fear. When I am around—'

'Yes, when you are around no one is likely to approach me,' Desirée agreed readily enough. 'But when you are not, what shall I do then? How am I to protect myself against the likes of Lord Perry and his friends?'

A sudden movement at the front door of the house drew Desirée's eye, and she abruptly caught her breath. Mrs Clyde was standing in the doorway, with Caroline on one side of her and the housekeeper at the other. And all three were staring directly across the field towards them.

'I have tarried too long,' Desirée said anxiously. 'I must return to the house at once.'

Sebastian glanced in the direction of the house too, and frowned. 'Then I shall come with you. There is more that I would say to you, Desirée, and if necessary, I shall introduce myself to your employer and—'

'No, it is best that you leave now, my lord. Mrs Clyde does not allow the staff to have visitors at the house. I shall go back and make my explanations as best I can.'

'Damn it, Desirée, I am not a visitor and I have no wish to go—'

'But you have no reason to stay either,' Desirée told him, feeling as though her heart was being wrenched in two. 'I...thank you for coming, but now that the question as to why I left London has been answered, there is no reason for you to remain.

Please, go back to London, my lord. Your staying here now can do neither of us any good.'

Desirée whirled around before he had a chance to say anything more and ran all the way back to the house. What a fool she had been. What a silly, ignorant fool to think that Sebastian Moore might have ever truly cared for her. The apprehension she felt over the coming interview with Mrs Clyde was nothing compared to the emptiness she felt at his cruel betrayal.

Oh yes, he had come to Yorkshire looking for her. But only to find out the truth of the matter with regards to Lord Perry. He thought no better of her now than he had on the day he'd met her in the river. If he had, he would *never* have believed what Lord Perry had said. He would not have blamed her for what had happened.

Well, she would not be so foolish in the future, Desirée assured herself. She refused to allow any man to reduce her to such a state again. She had let it happen once by being stupid enough to fall in love with Sebastian Moore.

She would not be so careless a second time.

Chapter Twelve

Mrs Clyde did not waste any time in telling Desirée exactly what she thought of her conduct.

'I am shocked at your behaviour, Miss Nash,' she said after summoning Desirée to her private parlour immediately upon her return to the house. 'I look out of my window to see my governess talking to a strange man in the field, while my daughters are left to make their own way back to the house? What am I to make of such conduct?'

'We were only in the pasture, Mrs Clyde.'

'I don't care if you were in the garden, Miss Nash!' the woman snapped. 'Your responsibility is to my children, not to your fancy gentlemen friends. I will not have my staff behaving in such a disgraceful manner!'

'Do you wish me to leave?' Desirée asked, not at all sure that she wouldn't be relieved if the woman *were* to dismiss her.

But Mrs Clyde only shook her head. 'Unfortunately, my wishes are not the only ones to be considered here. My girls have taken to you and it is *their* wish, Sarah's in particular, that you remain. For their sakes alone, I shall allow it. But you will be confined to the house for the next three weeks, Miss Nash, and I warn you, if anything like this should happen again, you will be turned off immediately and without a reference. Is that understood?'

'Yes, Mrs Clyde.'

'Good. You may go.'

Desirée inclined her head and turned to leave as anger and resentment welled up inside.

'Thank you, Sebastian,' she muttered under her breath as she headed for the nursery. 'It seems that you have brought me to the edge of grief once more.'

Sebastian sat in the bar at the Three Crowns and stared morosely into his glass. It had all gone wrong. Everything he had come here to do had gone abysmally wrong. And he had no one to blame but himself.

Why hadn't he trusted Desirée? Surely he'd known enough of her character to know that she would never have *agreed* to a relationship with Perry. And if she *had* ended up in one, it would only have been because he had coerced her in some way. Desirée was not the type of woman to involve herself in an *affaire de coeur* with such a loathsome man.

And yet, when he had finally caught up with her this afternoon and had been given an opportunity to talk to her, what had he done but let her believe that that was *exactly* what he had thought. Why had he not just asked her to tell him what had happened without imposing any opinions of his own?

And on top of all that, it was very possible that he had cost Desirée her job. He had seen the look on

Mrs Clyde's face when she had stood in the doorway and glared at them. And he knew what Desirée would have had to face when she walked back into that house. But what was he to do now? Go back to London? Leave Desirée to her miserable existence here? Because Sebastian knew that's what it was. Her carefully worded answers hadn't disguised the truth for a minute. She might care for one of the young girls in her care but there was certainly no affection or respect for the master or his wife.

Sebastian signalled for another drink and remembered again Lord Perry's smug complacency. God, when he thought about what the bastard had done, he felt like killing him. He could only imagine how Desirée must have felt at being trapped in a room with such a man and knowing what he intended to do— what he *would* have done had it not been for a most timely interruption.

But then, at the same time, how humiliated Desirée must have felt at being discovered by Mrs Guarding herself; a woman she admired and respected. And then to be dismissed by that same woman for conduct that had nothing to do with her and everything to do with a rich, powerful man who selfishly used others for his own pleasure and amusement.

How can I go back to London, knowing what I do now? Desirée had told him. *How could I…walk into a room with Lady Charlton, and hold my head up, knowing that half the gentlemen in the room are seeing me as Lord Perry does? Wondering, perhaps, if I would agree to be their mistress, if I would not be his—or yours?*

Hearing again the despair in her voice, Sebastian abruptly got up and began to pace. He could not bear the thought of *anyone* thinking of Desirée in such a manner. Making a mockery of all that she was. Ignoring her gentleness and compassion, and seeing her only as a beautiful woman to be used and bedded.

All right, damn it, so that was what he had once thought too, but those were not his feelings any more! Desirée would never be just that to him. Because if he was ever fortunate enough to have her in his bed, it would be because he wanted *all* of her. Not just her body, but her mind, her spirit, and her intellect as well.

Then tell her that, you fool, the voice said in his head. *Tell her and be done with it.*

Sebastian abruptly stopped pacing. Yes, of course that's what he would do. He would go back to that dreadful house tomorrow and he would demand to see her. And when he did, he would get down on his knees and beg her to forgive him.

He hoped to God that it wasn't already too late.

Sebastian called at Banksburgh House at precisely eleven o'clock the following morning. He knew that he was calling in advance of the socially accepted time, but he could not believe that in such a dismal place the niceties would be adhered to. Besides, the wait had already tried his patience sorely enough.

He was met at the door by a dour-faced butler who informed him that the master was not at home. When Sebastian presented his card and told him that he wished to see the lady of the house, he was grudgingly admitted to a chilly, cavernous hall and asked to wait. Moments later, he found himself being led into a large, cheerless drawing-room, where he was greeted by an obsequious Mrs Clyde.

'Lord Buckworth, I am honoured by your call,' she said, visibly flustered by his unexpected arrival. 'Most honoured indeed.'

'I hope I am not calling too early, Mrs Clyde.'

'Not at all, my lord. We do not keep town hours here. We rise very early at Banksburgh House. Can I offer you some refreshment?'

Sebastian politely inclined his head as he removed his leather gloves. 'Thank you, no. This is not entirely a social call. In fact, I have come on another matter altogether.'

'My lord?'

'I wish to see your governess.'

'I…beg your pardon?'

Sebastian smiled at her look of astonishment. 'Yes, you heard me correctly, Mrs Clyde. I wish to speak to Miss Nash. I believe you saw me talking to her in the field yesterday afternoon.'

'Well, yes, I did, but—'

'By the by, I apologize for sending your two lovely daughters back to the house without her,' Sebastian said before the woman had a chance to continue. 'Miss Nash was most upset at my doing so, but what I had to say to her was for her hearing alone. And I thought that with the house being within such easy distance there would be no problem.'

'Well, no, of course not, Lord Buckworth, however—'

'Good. I am relieved to hear it,' Sebastian interrupted smoothly. 'I should not like to think that Miss Nash was reprimanded for something that was not her fault. And now, if you would be so good as to send for the young lady, Mrs Clyde, I will trouble you no more.'

* * *

Desirée was in the nursery when the housekeeper arrived. She frowned at being told that Mrs Clyde wanted to see her in the drawing-room straight away, and wondered what she had done wrong now. Surely her employer had not changed her mind and decided to turn her off as a result of what had happened yesterday?

'Thank you, Mrs Hagerty. I shall go down at once.'

'Can I come too, Miss Nash?' Sarah asked innocently.

In spite of her concerns, Desirée managed a smile for the little girl. 'No, Sarah, not this time. I think your mama wishes to speak with me alone.'

'Don't know about that,' the housekeeper said in a broad Yorkshire accent. 'There's already a fine London gentleman with her.'

Desirée blanched. A *London* gentleman? But... surely Sebastian had not come back? Not after what had passed between them yesterday?

Her nerves in a flutter, Desirée quickly made her way downstairs. Perhaps Sebastian had called out of respect and Mrs Clyde had summoned her downstairs to remind her again of the impropriety of her actions. Certainly that seemed a more logical explanation.

Desirée nervously smoothed down the front of her ugly brown dress and then knocked on the drawing-room door. Upon being told to enter, she pushed it open and walked in. The first person she saw was Sebastian. He was immaculately dressed and was leaning nonchalantly against the mantle. It seemed to Desirée that his eyes were bright with merriment.

Mrs Clyde, on the other hand, was looking somewhat bewildered as she sat in her usual chair beside the fireplace, her gown of puce-coloured silk clashing hideously with her auburn hair.

'You wished to see me, Mrs Clyde.'

'Yes, Miss Nash, I did. We have been honoured by a visit from this fine gentleman, but you can imagine my surprise when he told me that he wished to see *you*.'

'Good morning, Miss Nash,' Sebastian said with a bow.

'Lord Buckworth.' Desirée greeted him politely.

'I was just explaining to Mrs Clyde the circumstances of our meeting yesterday,' he informed her. 'I assured her that the blame for it *and* for sending the children back unescorted was entirely mine and that you should not be held in any way responsible. Is that not so, Mrs Clyde?'

'It is, Lord Buckworth. And while I was most upset with Miss Nash for her conduct yesterday, I am willing to admit—now that I have met you—that I made a mistake. At the time, of course, I was most concerned for the welfare of my girls, and that is what Miss Nash is here for, after all.'

'Your concern for your daughters' welfare does you proud, Mrs Clyde,' Sebastian assured her. 'But now that you are more comfortable with my presence, perhaps you would be so good as to allow me a few moments alone with Miss Nash?'

The woman's smile slipped. 'Well, it is not entirely proper, Lord Buckworth—'

'I promise you that I shall be the soul of propriety, Mrs Clyde. You see, I come with news about a very dear friend of Miss Nash's, and it is of a somewhat...delicate and personal nature. As such, I would not wish to embarrass her by making it known in front of others. You understand.'

Not looking as though she did, but obviously unwilling to say so in front of this man, Mrs Clyde reluctantly got to her feet. 'Very well, Lord Buckworth. You may have a few moments alone with Miss Nash. But then I must return her to her duties. I am sure you understand that my girls require constant supervision. Especially my eldest daughter, Caroline,' she said pointedly. 'A pretty little thing, did you not think, Lord Buckworth?'

'I did indeed, Mrs Clyde. And no doubt she will be breaking hearts when she makes her come-out in four or five years time. No doubt just like her mama did when she made hers.'

Desirée pressed her lips together to keep from smiling. Truly, Sebastian was outrageous! Mrs Clyde was blushing like a schoolgirl. But his flattery was obviously achieving the desired results.

'You are too kind, my dear Lord Buckworth,' the woman said as she headed for the door. 'Pray, enjoy your visit with Miss Nash.'

As soon as the door closed behind her, Sebastian let out his breath. 'Good God, for a moment there I thought she was going to kiss me.'

'It would have served you right if she had,' Desirée replied tartly.

'Miss Nash, I am wounded that you would speak to me in such a manner,' Sebastian said, feigning injury. 'I came here today in an effort to clear your good name and to make sure you were not taken to task over what happened, and this is the thanks I receive?'

'Your good intentions are much appreciated, my

lord, but I am afraid they arrive somewhat late. I have already been chastised for my wanton behaviour.'

'Is that what she called it?'

'That was what she *would* have called it, had she bothered to put a name to it.'

Sebastian quickly smothered a smile. 'Dear me. Then what you're saying is that I needn't have been so ingratiating in my address today.'

'No, but I am sure it sent her off in a sweeter temper than she would have gone otherwise.' Uncertain of what to do next, Desirée walked towards the couch and sat down. 'But pray, what brings you back here this morning? I thought you would have been well on your way to London by now.'

'I could not go back to London and leave you here, Desirée. Surely you know that.'

His voice had lost its teasing quality and turned infinitely gentle—and Desirée hardened her heart against it. 'I know nothing of the sort, my lord. Why should I?'

'Because I was a fool,' Sebastian said as he sat down beside her. 'I owe you an apology, Desirée. I thought long and hard about what you told me yesterday. And I realised, in my heart, that I didn't believe Perry for a moment when he intimated that you and he had been involved.'

'That is not what you led me to believe yesterday.'

'No. Because it wasn't until last night that I realised my reaction to Lord Perry was motivated by jealousy rather than anger.'

Desirée gasped. 'You were…jealous?'

'Outrageously,' Sebastian admitted. 'Even the thought of him being that close to you disturbed me to such an extent that I lost the ability to see the situation rationally. You mean more to me than it is possible for me to express in words, Desirée, and I am so deeply sorry that I hurt you.'

His eyes were filled with such tenderness and compassion that Desirée felt tears well in her own. 'My lord, I—'

'No, let me finish. It was never my intention to hurt you, Desirée. After that day in the river, I never imagined that I would see you again. You were like…a beautiful dream; someone I could think about, but never have. And yes, when I got back to London, I did tell someone that I had met you. But what I said to him was not in any way improper or obscene. I did not tell him what you were wearing or suggest that you behaved in a loose or wanton manner. If he drew those conclusions from what I said, then all I can do is apologise for his misinterpretation. But I can assure you that I said nothing of the kind.'

'You did not say that I was naked?'

'No. In fact, I did not refer to your physical appearance at all, other than to say that you were an extremely beautiful young woman. And though I am not trying to assign blame for what happened, I think it only right to tell you that Lord Perry is actually the one who betrayed you.'

Desirée's eyes widened in dismay. 'How do you know?'

'He told me as much a few days ago. He said he knew that you were partial to swimming in the river, and that when he heard Lord Hutchings's version of the story, he assumed it had to be you. But if it is of any comfort at all, I do not think as many people know that you were my delightful water nymph as he might have led you to believe. I think that was part of his plan for making you agree to become his mistress.'

Desirée felt the blush creep up into her cheeks. 'I suppose, in all fairness, I should not be so quick to condemn you for telling a friend when I have already admitted to telling one of my own.'

'Ah yes, the young lady who shared her knowledge of my…reputation with you.'

Desirée's colour heightened. 'Perhaps. But it is *because* of what Helen said that I wrote to you in the first place.'

'And what I know now, that I didn't know then, was that you wrote that letter because of what Lord Perry had done to you,' Sebastian said gently, 'and what it necessitated you doing in return.'

'Yes. I did not see that I had any choice,' Desirée said, knowing there was little point in prevaricating now. 'Mrs Guarding was very sorry to have to dismiss me but she had no choice either. There was very little likelihood that word of what had happened would not make its way around the school. And if it were to reach the village and beyond, the reputation of the school might have suffered. So, I thought about my choices and realised there was no possibility of respectable employment in the villages, and, in my highly distraught state, I thought about you and…what you had offered that day in the pool.'

Sebastian looked down into her face and shook his head. 'It must have been terribly difficult for you to write such a letter.'

'It was. But when I considered all of my options, I truly could not see…any other way out,' Desirée admitted softly. 'I had to leave Steep Abbot, for I knew there would always be a stigma attached to my name. And Helen had told me that you were a good man, so I acted on impulse and sent you the letter.'

'So in a way, I have Helen to thank for all of this.'

'In a way.' Desirée glanced up at him and smiled. 'Had she told me you were a brute, I would certainly not have written it.'

'But you did, and it started us upon a journey that neither of us expected to end here.'

Desirée sighed. 'No, my lord, certainly *I* did not.'

Hesitating, Sebastian took her right hand in his and stared down at it. 'Something else became clear to me last night, Desirée. Something which has been on my mind for some time now. Indeed, since long before I went away to Hertfordshire.' He raised his eyes to hers and knew in his heart that what he was doing was right. 'I want you to come back to London with me, Desirée. My life has been so empty without you and I need you back in it. I want us to ride together in the park and to dance the night away. I want you in my life, Aphrodite.'

Desirée's smile abruptly faded. For one heart-stopping moment, she had thought that Sebastian was about to offer her marriage—until he had called her Aphrodite. Then, she'd known. That was the name he had used when they had first met and when she was to have been his mistress. Obviously, that was what he wanted again.

She slowly withdrew her hand and stood up. 'I am…sorry, Lord Buckworth, I cannot return to London with you.'

'But…why not?'

'I have already told you. Nothing would change. Everyone would look at me exactly the same way they do now. The only difference would be that the men would leave me alone knowing that I was your mistress—'

'My mistress!' Sebastian's face darkened as he also got to his feet. 'Is that what you think this is all about? That I am asking you to come back to London as my *mistress*?'

'Well, what else was I to think? You said that…you wanted me in your life, and that we should….ride together in the park and dance the night away. And then you called me Aphrodite.'

'Yes, and so you are and always shall be,' Sebastian said as he drew her close. 'But I want you beside me as my wife, Desirée, not as my mistress.'

'Your *wife*!' she gasped.

'Of course, you silly girl. I don't intend to have any man look at you in any way but with the respect due you as Viscountess Buckworth. I want them all to admire your beauty—but only from a distance. And I shall challenge *any* man who is foolish enough to think he can take liberties with you. I want you as my wife and my lady, Desirée Nash.' Sebastian took her chin in his hand and gently tipped it back. 'Please tell me that I have not lost any hope of one day hearing you say that you love me.'

'Love you? Oh, my dearest Sebastian, now it is you who are being foolish,' Desirée cried. 'For I have been in love with you for such a very long time.'

With a muffled cry of joy, Sebastian pulled her into his arms. His mouth came down on hers and Desirée knew that she had finally come home. Here, in this man's arms, was where she was meant to be.

At length, Sebastian raised his head to look down into her sparkling green eyes. 'My sweet Aphrodite. When I think how close I came to losing you.'

'It would not have happened. *Quos amor verus tenuit, tenebit,*' Desirée quoted softly. 'To whom true love has held, it will go on holding.'

Sebastian smiled and brushed his lips lightly against hers. 'What other things do you intend to teach me, my beautiful bluestocking?'

'Only this. *Amor vincit omnia.*'

This time, there was a sparkle in Sebastian's eyes as his lips closed over hers again. 'How very appropriate,' he murmured huskily. 'Love conquers all. Well, if that is to be the nature of the lesson, my darling Desirée, I think I shall be only too happy to be the pupil!'

* * * * *

MILLS & BOON®

Makes any time special™

Mills & Boon publish 29 new titles every month. Select from...

Modern Romance™   **Tender Romance**™

Sensual Romance™

Medical Romance™   **Historical Romance**™

MAT2

A
Perfect Family

An enthralling family saga by bestselling author

PENNY JORDAN

Published 20th July